TEST DRIVE

WATCHERS CREW BOOK 1

INES JOHNSON

THOSE JOHNSON GIRLS

Copyright © 2015, Ines Johnson. All rights reserved.

All rights reserved. No part of this book may be reproduced, stored in a retrieval system, or transmitted in any form, or by any means, electronic, mechanical, photocopying, recording, or otherwise, without prior permission of the author.

Manufactured in the United States of America

ONE

I hadn't realized it was so late by the time I came out of the lab. The night was a thick cloak. The air humid and wet. But it pulsed with life. I heard crickets chirping. Beetles rustled leaves. Off in the distance, fireflies flashed their lights on and off like a beacon beckoning me to come deeper into the night. I put my head down and continued on towards the parking lot.

Nighttime and darkness weren't familiar to me. I'd grown up with a curfew to be inside before the street lamps came on. My entire life seemed timed around those man-made suns. As a kid, I left for school in the morning when the lights shut off. I was safe inside each night before they blinked back on again. The street lamp in the parking lot outside of the Biology building beamed brightly now.

"Ellie, wait up."

I turned at the sound of my name.

Shakira James made her way over to me. Her thick, gold-hooped earrings caught the streetlight and twinkled. She was a sophomore taking Biology 101. I'd been helping her prepare for finals. At the first glance of her mini skirt and halter top, I'd assumed we'd be starting from the beginning with the birds and the bees; the classifications of those organisms, not their mating habits. But it turned out Shakira had an excellent grasp of the basics. Her questions ventured more into the theories of evolution and natural selection.

"You think you could give me a ride, sis?"

I hesitated. I'd only known Shakira a few days. I assumed she would live on the bad side of town. Not because she was black -or was it politically correct to say African-American? My assumption wasn't based on her race, but more because her boobs spilled out of her top. Girls from good families didn't expose their underwear as part of their ensemble.

Then I caught myself. I had a habit of doing that; judging people based on their appearances. It was a habit I'd picked up in my field of study. As an entomologist I observed insects and made inferences based on those observations. It worked well with insects, but not so much with humans. I often found my foot shoved uncomfortably into my mouth when I addressed Homo Sapiens. I'd already assumed Shakira wasn't smart based on how she dressed. I was probably wrong again with her socioeconomic status. Maybe she was just a rebellious youth and her parents were pastors in an upper middle class neighborhood.

"Sure," I said.

We made our way over to my car. My patent leather shoes tapped the ground quietly as though to not disturb the asphalt. Shakira's stilettoed boots struck the pavement with an attitude that would've awakened the worms burrowed in the warm earth.

"Wow," Shakira said as I unlocked the doors of my car with the fob. "This is your ride, sis?"

I nodded, my chest swelling with pride inside my cardigan. I'd never been one to be flashy with my clothing or makeup. My car was my only statement piece.

"I guess it fits your personality." Shakira wrinkled her nose as she ducked inside.

I frowned unsure if she'd given me a compliment or not?

"I mean, I get it, sis." Shakira strapped on the seat belt. "You're studying to be an entomologist and you have a ladybug car."

My car was a red Volkswagen Beetle with black spots. Bugs had fascinated me since I'd seen an army of tiny ants lift a potato chip I'd dropped during a grade school picnic. Being petite myself, I wanted to understand how those small creatures managed such a hefty feat. My inquiry of ants led me down a rabbit's hole into an amazing, intricate, miniature world where the smallest creatures had the largest powers.

Shakira's directions took us away from campus. We headed away from the trendy market district, where most of the college students did their shopping and entertainment. We drove past the docks where many of the underclassmen who didn't work coalesced. We pulled up into a seedy part of town.

I doubted any pastor would set up a church on these outskirts. I clutched at the wheel as the streetlights became sparser, and some weren't lit at all. People were out on the streets. Young boys and grown men leered at the tween girls and grown women who walked by in skirts shorter than Shakira's.

"It's just over here." Shakira pointed to a one-way street with no houses. Lined up in the parking lot of an abandoned factory were rows upon rows of sleek cars.

"Where's your house?"

"Girl, I don't live in this jacked neighborhood. I'm just meeting this guy here." Shakira moved her hips side to side in the seat causing a squeaky sound.

I was sure Shakira's movements were unconscious, but it was a movement I'd observed before. Many insects let off a vibration by moving their legs together to indicate they were ready to mate. Outside the car, I could hear crickets strumming into the night air.

"Is he your boyfriend?"

Shakira didn't get that dreamy look that girls got when they thought about a guy they liked. Her face crunched into an expression between a grimace and a snicker. "He's not boyfriend material, sis. Just someone I'm hooking up with."

Her cavalier attitude shouldn't have shocked me. Most insects were not monogamous, not in the human sense of the word. Take the honeybee, for example. The queen had a ton of lovers at her beck and call to service her needs, and not one of the thousands of female worker bees in her kingdom would dare call her out of her name.

I'd had exactly one boyfriend during my twenty years and we had done little more than chaste kissing the year we'd been dating. We had gotten to second base over Spring Break. Though I think it may have been an accident on his part.

"Thanks for the ride, sis." Shakira did a quick application of lip-gloss in the vanity mirror.

I looked out the car window at the festivities. Someone had lit a fire in a trashcan. People were dancing around on the asphalt. Girls were shaking their barely covered behinds while guys leaned back on cars and watched.

"Is this someone's birthday party?" I asked.

Shakira cast me a side-glance. "It's a street race."

I looked out the window and saw no one in a tracksuit. Then I realized she must mean a *streetcar* race. I looked again at the line of cars in the lot.

"I'll see you on Monday, sis."

She didn't even think to invite me. Who was stereotyping who now? But she was right. This wasn't my scene. If I wasn't out with my boyfriend at a fancy restaurant, I spent my evenings watching reruns on the *National Geographic Channel*.

I watched Shakira switch her hips up to a group of guys. She wasn't the only woman sashaying around them. In the middle of all the bare skin was what I could only describe as a magnet. I tried to look away from him, but my eyes caught on his muscles, which seemed to burst through his blue mechanic's shirt that had the sleeves cut off. My eyes latched onto his close-cut hair, which reminded me of Vin Diesel in that racing movie; my only reference to or experience with street racing. This magnet of a man was deeply tanned, not brown-skinned, but not white either. I wasn't good with identifying other cultures having grown up lily white. But he looked exotic to me.

He was surrounded by three other guys; all three were big with muscles. They were a United Nations of colors. They reminded me of the United Colors of Benetton ads from when I was a kid.

The guy closest to the magnet was black. Or should I say African-American? I wished I'd asked Shakira, but she'd probably look at me with that side-eyed glance again. Unlike the diesel god standing next to him, the black guy had a bald head. He was laughing at something a blond-haired Adonis said. The Adonis would put Paul Walker to shame with his blue eyes and dimples. I watched as Shakira sauntered up to the Asian guy who rounded out the group. The Asian's muscles were sleek and honed. His dark eyes watched her with silent intent.

My hand rested on the gearshift, which was still in the P for park position. The streetlight blinked on over top of me casting me in a spot light. The Diesel-magnet looked up at the blinking light. Then tilted his head down and found me.

I expected his eyes to look away, but they didn't. They caught and held. He tilted his head to the side, looking at me as though... interested.

My breath caught in my throat under his dark gaze. I gulped. My legs rubbed together, the friction heating me. A wetness bloomed in my panties, behind my knees, in my palms. The Diesel-magnet's eyes narrowed as though he could tell what was happening with the increased fluid levels all over my body.

He tilted his head in the other direction, eyes still on me. I watched his lips move. Shakira leaned over to him. She looked back, at me. They both stared a second. Then she spoke to him. Her motions were dismissive. I was sure she was telling him I wasn't worth his time, that I was an inconsequential girl, probably racist, definitely sheltered, who stayed in the back of a lab marveling over insects and creepy crawlies.

Having given him her estimation of me, Shakira looked away. But he didn't. A slow smile spread across his face as he held me there in my car under the glaring light. His tongue snuck out of his mouth and he licked his slips, slow. First the pink tip traced the upper lip. It climbed the hill of the fleshy region, dipped into the deep crevice in the center, and then began the descent down to the bottom lip.

I sat there frozen under his gaze, watching his tongue, transfixed.

Until he turned away.

I hadn't noticed he'd been leaning against a car; a black Charger. I only knew that because it was the same car that Vin Diesel drove in that string of movies. Diesel's look-alike turned away from me. His attention focused on another girl. His hands, along with the black guy and the blond guy's hands, felt up the girl. They didn't take turns. They all mauled her at once, but she didn't appear to mind. She looked like she reveled in the attention.

Without another look at me, he hopped into the driver's seat of the muscle car. The other guys followed suit, hopping into other muscle cars of various makes and models. They all lined up for what I assumed was the race.

A girl in scanty shorts held a scarf up in the air in front of all the cars. I watched the scarf drop and the cars take off. They roared past me in a stampede going the wrong way down the one-way street. The street light above me blinked. The lot emptied out after them and I was left alone in the darkness.

TWO

Long after the lot emptied, I sat there in the darkness. My heart pounding after the roar of those engines had long since receded. My slick thighs stuck together from the sight of that thick tongue tracing those full lips while looking at me.

No one had ever looked at me like that, not even Jerry, my boyfriend. People rarely looked at me at all. All my life I'd felt like a firefly that only came out during the day. There was nothing remarkable about shining your light under the dazzling rays of the sun. But when he'd stared at me, it was like he knew that there was a spark in me; a spark that no one could see because I was so often standing in the light of day and safely tucked away when night fell.

But not tonight.

Tonight I was out in the thick of it. The party was louder than crickets chirping or beetles rustling leaves. I heard people laughing. I heard the loud music. Everything in the surrounding darkness pulsed with life. It thrummed through me, shaking something loose. I had the inclination to reach for the door handle and step out into the night, to step out of myself. To shed the skin I'd been cocooned inside and shake free my newfound wings and fly.

A beeping sound broke me from my trance. I snatched my hand away from the door handle and picked up my phone. It was a text message from Jerry. "Can't wait to see you next weekend," it said.

Right. *Next weekend.*

I sighed and put my phone away. We'd been planning *next weekend* for a while now. Jerry and I had been dating for almost a year. He'd never pressured me, not once, about sex. So, I was shocked last week when he brought up the idea of a weekend away together. He'd clarified that he would like to engage in intercourse with me.

He'd said it just like that. "Ellie, I'd like for you to entertain the idea of intercourse with me."

It hadn't made me rub my thighs together like a cricket in heat. But I felt it was time. Our relationship had progressed along as though we'd ticked off an updated Victorian courting calendar.

Our courtship had begun with several dates. A handshake ended the first, a hug the second, a chaste kiss on the cheek for the third. Jerry hadn't migrated to a kiss on my lips until after a month of dates. He hadn't used his tongue for another two months. I'd met his parents during Thanksgiving and he met mine over Christmas. And then there was the boob grazing over Spring Break. It had taken a long time to reach third base, and though my knees weren't making music, I found myself eager to cross over the home plate.

I texted Jerry back a smiley face. Not the one with the hearts in its eyes. Not the one blowing kisses. Just the plain standard smile.

The streetlight above me blinked back on to its full light, taking me out of the darkness and back into full light. I looked up at the cleared lot. The onlookers of the race were likely going to wherever the end point was.

I thought about following them. I considered heading over to the end point of the race, getting out of my car, and standing out in the darkness. Stepping into the glare of head beams, so he could see me again. Maybe take his tongue around the track of his lips again. Maybe he'd blow me another kiss and ignite me with more than a look. I was sure girls sent him all kinds of suggestive emojis along with a string of heart-shaped kisses.

I looked down at myself. My skirt came down past my knees. My shoes were flats with no spike. I had on two layers of shirts; a camisole and a long sleeve cardigan. I caught my reflection in the rear view mirror. My blonde hair was pulled back in a ponytail that looked childish suddenly. I shut my blue eyes, pulled the gear into drive, and headed down the proper direction of the one-way street. I reached the end of the street only to realize that I did not know where I was going.

I took a left, but that street looked unfamiliar.

I took a right, but felt as though I were going in circles. This part of the neighborhood looked even rougher than the parking lot.

I heard a loud roar behind me. I saw headlights getting closer and closer. I realized I was in the line of the race. I pulled my Bug over to the curb, but heard a loud pop and felt a bump. Dread crawled up my back when I realized I'd blown a tire.

Four cars zoomed past me. Once they passed, I got out of my car to confirm that I had rolled over broken glass and my tire was indeed flat. There was a blinking streetlight above me. I pulled out my phone to see I had one bar of service out in this satellite tower desert.

Great.

I was stuck out in the middle of nowhere with no help in sight. I was a wiz at identifying bugs and insects, but I had no clue how to change a tire.

I reached into the passenger side dashboard for the car manual. Surely, there were instructions on how to change a tire. I was great at textbook directions. I opened the book, but the sound of wheels coming closer brought my attention up.

THREE

Four cars pulled up in front of me in a choreographed move I'd only seen in car commercials. My heart thudded in my ears to think I'd be meeting my end in a rank part of town. But more troubling than my imminent demise was the thought that my beautiful car would likely be stripped down for its parts.

My heart didn't slow down in relief when the Vin Diesel look-alike emerged from the driver's side of the Charger. It beat out an entirely different pattern.

"Hey," he called. His voice was deeper than the action star's baritone. It grumbled in the same octave of his muscle car. "You all right, little girl?"

I blinked. Little girl? I didn't look *that* young. I was twenty, nearly twenty-one. Definitely legal. I'd been on my own for four years now, and I'd just bought this car with my own money and no help from my parents.

Sure, my place was in a college dorm. And okay, so maybe I didn't know how to take care of my vehicle in terms of changing a tire. But that didn't make me an adolescent.

"I'm fine," I said crossing my arms over my shoulders in child-like defiance.

I felt four pairs of eyes zero in on my chest. I brought my hands down to my sides.

"It's just a little car trouble." My voice wobbled under their stares. "My boyfriend will be here shortly to help."

"Boyfriend?" Diesel's eyes held a challenge.

It was as though he saw inside of me; saw Jerry. This powerful man before me bent down and looked in my mind, saw my image of Jerry, looked him up and down, found my boyfriend wanting, and dismissed him all with a curl of his full lips.

Then he looked down at the driver's manual in my hand. His grin spread wider. He reached out his hand. It was a massive paw, like what I'd imagine a lion's would look like up close. My head would fit easily in his palm with space to turn right or left and snuggle. He held out his giant, open palm and flicked his fingers in a beckoning motion. Something about the movement made me press my thighs together.

"Give it here," he commanded.

I did as I was told. I handed him the manual.

He tossed the manual back into my car. It landed on the passenger seat with a thud.

"Eagle, Crow, come take a look at this."

I watched two other huge figures march over. It was the black guy and the blond Adonis with the dimpled grin. Their eyes were on me. My heart beat so fast it skidded around the cavity of my chest. The disturbance clanged so loud the vibrations pulsed in between my thighs.

The size of these men was overwhelming. I thought of Jerry with his lanky height. I'd seen him with his shirt off a handful of times when we were at the beach over Spring Break. He wasn't flabby, but he didn't have the definition I saw through these guys' tight shirts.

I should be freaking out right now. There were three massive guys surrounding me, and a fourth, the Asian one, leaned against one of the cars just watching it all go down.

Then I remembered, that guy, the Asian guy watching, he was Shakira's boyfriend or hookup or whatever. Surely they wouldn't do anything to me if they knew I knew her. Or at least not if I could identify them in police photos. That is, if they left me alive.

"It looks like a blow," said the black guy.

"Yeah, looks like it," confirmed the blond one.

"She was trying to read the manual on how to fix it," the Diesel magnet chuckled. His eyes never left my face. "You shouldn't be out here by yourself. A piece of sweet meat like you would get eaten up real quick."

There was something in the way he said it that made the experience sound anything but scary. He smiled as though he sensed I wasn't afraid. I felt like he was testing me, and surprisingly, it looked like I was passing the examination.

"My boys'll change the tire for you. Be quicker than waiting for your boyfriend to come and get you."

"My boyfriend's not coming." I blinked at my honest stupidity.

He quirked an eyebrow.

"I don't even think he knows how to change a tire. I just said that so you wouldn't think I was all alone."

"But you are all alone."

"Not anymore," I said. "I doubt anybody will bother with me while you four are around."

"You think we won't... bother with you?" He stepped in closer.

I'd become excellent at observation over my years of studying insects under microscopes and in their natural habitats. I understood what the most minuscule of movements could mean. I watched this guy's pupils dilate in the darkness. I watched him inhale his big chest to capacity. He straightened his broad shoulders bringing himself up to his full height. He was making himself appear bigger, trying to scare me away. The curious nerd in me wanted to understand why.

I shook my head in answer to his question. "No. I don't think you'll bother with me. You would've already done that if you wanted to. You wouldn't be fixing up my getaway vehicle right now if you wanted to do me harm. You're trying to scare me at the same time as you're giving me a way out."

His face lit up like a game board. He stepped into me, leaving me barely an inch of personal space. My butt bumped against the car door.

"You're wrong, sweet meat. I *am* going to bother with you."

He ran his fingers lightly across my forearm. My

breath came out in tiny gasps at the sparks of electricity that ran across my arm where his fingers barely touched, raising the hairs there. Two of his thick fingers rested on my pulse at the end of my wrist. The beat raced a million miles per second.

He continued down and unfurled my fingers. I heard a jangling sound. He freed my car keys from my clenched palm and tossed them to the two guys standing at the rear of my car.

I looked over my shoulder to see the two big guys leaning against my trunk watching the entire exchange. Their gazes were hungry, but patient. My pulse sped even faster. For the first time tonight, I saw I was in real danger.

The black guy came to the front of the car, popped the hood, and took out the tire from its compartment in the Beetle. He went back around and joined the white guy and then the two bent down and got to work. I turned my attention back to the man before me. He smiled down at me, still watching my every move. Still trying to see if I would scare away.

"Aren't you guys missing the race?" I asked.

"I won the race ten minutes ago," he said. "I always win. We were headed back to collect the winnings when I saw you on the side of the road."

He leaned his forearm on the hood of my car, trapping me in on one side. "You know you're gonna have to pay for this tire change."

"Of course." I made to turn around to grab my purse, but he stopped my hand on the car door.

"I don't want your money."

"What do you want?"

"Two kisses."

"Kisses?" I frowned. "From me?"

He nodded.

"Why? Why would you want to kiss...me?"

"You ever been kissed before, sweet meat?"

I frowned at the name he kept calling me, certain it was an insult that I didn't understand. Then I thought about his question.

Jerry and I kissed. Lots of times. They were really nice kisses. I looked forward to them, especially now that he was using his tongue.

"I'm gonna take that as a no if you have to think about it that hard," he said. "And if you haven't been kissed properly, I'm going to take it that you've never come before."

I felt the blood rush to my cheeks. I knew he saw my embarrassment in the dim light. But I also knew he was trying to rile me up again, trying to scare me away. He only blocked me in on one side. I could escape if I wanted to. He was toying with me like a predator did his prey.

"Untouched and curious. Fresh, sweet meat just waiting to be lit on fire." He practically purred. "You're exactly my type."

A small group of fireflies glowed in the distance approaching us in the dark street. The street lamp flickered off at that moment, casting us into dark shadows.

"How about it? Will you let me kiss you? Two times? I promise it will be done properly and thoroughly."

He was giving me a choice. I could say *no* if I wanted to. I pressed my legs together. My one knee slicked off the other from the dampness that had gathered from his proximity and suggestions. The light above us blinked again, on and then off, casting us in bright light and then darkness.

The light blinked out again, leaving only the moon's glow. With the night to cover me, I tilted my head up in answer.

FOUR

It was just a kiss -two kisses.

Two proper kisses all at once. He'd probably use tongue. No, he'd definitely use his tongue. And probably not just a chaste flick across my lips, or a tentative swipe at my tongue. He'd go all in. No waiting for months. No minding some long ago courting calendar.

Two kisses from a guy I wasn't likely to see ever again after tonight.

Why not?

I was out in the dark. No one would see. No one would know. He could be my big, dark secret that I thought about from time to time when the lights were all out, and I was in my three-story home, with my two kids, and my one husband. I could think back and remember the time I kissed that guy... I didn't even know his name.

I was about to ask him when he leaned in a fraction. He hovered above me, not touching me, not not-touching me either. His fingers whispered over the hairs on my wrists. His lips hovered over mine until only a layer of breath existed between us.

"Fuck, sweet meat. You want it bad, don't you? You need it."

He was right. I did. I didn't know how bad I needed it until this very moment. This feeling of excitement. This feeling of my pulse racing. This feeling of freedom that was available in the middle of the night.

All my life things came to me easily. I got good grades. I got into the college of my choice. My career studies came easily. The perfect guy for me showed up one day and asked me out.

Everything was going according to some plan written out in a manual for good girls that I had never cracked open. I had never said this was the life I wanted. I'd never been given the opportunity to choose.

Until now.

He hovered over me. Waiting. Watching.

I leaned into him. I felt the denim of his pants

brush against my exposed knees and felt completely naked. I let out a whimper. And, as though that were his cue, his tongue slipped out of his mouth. That same tongue I'd watched trace around his lips as he'd looked at me like he wanted me, like he wanted to do the same to me.

And then he was doing the same to me. His tongue traced the outline of my upper lips. It climbed the hill that was the right side of my mouth, rested in the divot at the top, and made a slow descent down.

His tongue was warm, wet. He only gave me the tip, and he only gave it lightly. I felt disappointed that he went no further than my boyfriend.

Then I felt him smile against my lips as though that had been another test. I must've gotten that challenge right too because I felt his breath enter me as he traced the pattern of my desire across the underside of my lip. He sucked that spot behind the divot at the crest of my upper lip.

I opened wider, signaling he could take more.

He didn't.

He reached the corner of one side of my mouth, then changed the direction of his tongue and slowly swept the bottom of my lip. I was trembling by the time he got to the center.

He took small licks, like he was licking up the drippings of an ice cream cone. God, was I drooling?

He was almost at the other end when a devastating thought hit me. He's about to finish. When he reached the other corner of my mouth he'd be finished and it would be over. I wanted to launch a formal protest. This wasn't a kiss, not a real, proper kiss.

No sooner than I thought it did he pull away. I groaned in protest, lurching after him. He didn't go far. I lost my balance and crashed into his chest.

He put his thumb under my chin and lifted my face to his. There was a spark of triumph on his handsome face. "Was that a yes?"

I frowned. "A yes to what?"

"Being kissed."

"You mean? You mean that wasn't the first kiss?"

He laughed. "Baby if that's what you think a proper kiss is then you need to dump your boyfriend."

He pushed my hips back into the car with a thud. Not rough, but not gentle either. He boxed me in this time, both hands caging me in. Without warning his mouth came down on mine. There was no preamble. His tongue swept into my mouth and set about claiming every corner of my being.

His body pressed into mine. His hands pushed me into the driver's side window of my Bug. His hips pushed me against the door. And, oh god, I felt his erection at my belly. I'd never understood that when I read it in romance novels. Wouldn't the heroine feel the hero's erection pressed against her thigh when they kissed? Nope, not when the hero was well endowed and erect.

My legs pressed together as more arousal leaked out of me. He lifted me up into the air, just a foot off the ground. When I came back down his knee was right in between my thighs, right where I needed it to be.

I gasped at the impact of sensations. Then I groaned. I'd broken the kiss. Did that mean I only had one left?

His mouth was on mine again. His hand was in my hair, fingers digging into the base of my skull. He gave a tug arching my head back and delving even further with his tongue. His other hand rested just under my breast. I couldn't decide where to concentrate.

He rubbed his knee between my thighs in a circular motion. Then I realized that wasn't him making that tight circle. That was me. I was shamelessly humping the leg of a man, a street racer, whose name I didn't know, out in the middle of the night, in the middle of the street.

"Fuck, you need it, don't you? So fucking sweet. That's it; rub your sweet cunt on my knee. Get your juices on me."

His words were a punch to my gut. I should be offended that he'd said the C-word. It was disgusting, dirty -and I loved it.

I sat down on his knee then, trying to relieve the sweet pressure that was building there. He was right; I'd never had an orgasm before. Jerry hadn't ever tried to go down there. I'd never touched myself.

Now all of my attention was focused on that spot. I was going to do it. I was going to have my first orgasm. I was going to come, from my cunt, right out on the street.

The clanging of metal jerked me back to my senses.

"Fuck, Crow," he said. "Seriously? Can you handle your goddamn tool?"

I hopped down off the knee between my legs and closed my thighs. I'd completely forgotten we'd had an audience. I couldn't see the two guys fixing my wheel, but I'd heard them. On the other side of the street I saw the Asian guy still leaning against his car in the same pose, eyes still watching me with cool interest.

What had I been thinking? I'd gotten so hot and bothered I'd nearly let a group of guys see me orgasm.

FIVE

"What's the matter, sweet meat?"

The man before me had removed his knee from between my legs, but he still had his body pressed up against mine. He held my chin in his thumb and forefinger, bringing my face and attention around to him.

"My name's Ellie."

"You still owe me another kiss, Ellie. Or did you change your mind?"

I hadn't changed my mind. I wanted that second kiss. Just not so public. "Could we... go somewhere?"

"I don't know you, Ellie. You could take advantage of me in some dark corner if I went off with you."

It was so ludicrous I laughed in his face. I was

120 pounds in heavy boots and a parka. He had to be at least 220 of muscle and bulk.

He ran his fingers over my brow. His eyes looked at me in wonder. "Man, you're so fucking sweet. Let me have another taste of you, Ellie?"

"What about your friends?"

"My boys? They won't touch you unless you invite them to. We like our women willing. Personally, I like them begging for it."

"But they can see."

"That bothers you?"

I could see it was another of his challenges.

"You were about to come, weren't you Ellie? Your heart was racing, your blood was pumping. And that was before you remembered they were there. When you realized they were there your heart rate sped up even more, didn't it?" He ran his hands over my racing pulse. "Imagine how hard you'll come with that thought in the back of your mind." He grinned in mock sadness. "Wait, you can't imagine it because you've never come before."

And then he stepped away from me.

I nearly fell after him.

"Tell me you want it, Ellie. Tell me you want to come."

"I..."

He watched me again, trying to see if he could intimidate me. Trying to see if he could make me flee. But I saw it in his eyes, he wanted me to stay. He desperately wanted it.

I wanted it too.

"You gotta ask for it, baby."

"I...," I stammered. "I don't know your name."

He smiled. I felt like prey caught in his trap. "It's Hawk."

"Will you make me come please, Hawk?"

The streetlight came on full bright. The look on his face was brighter. "So. Fucking. Sweet."

He boxed me in against the car again. He was on me with a deeper hunger this time. I tried to get my hips closer to his. I even lifted my leg. He caught my thigh in his massive hand and hooked it over his hip. Then he did the same with the other. He angled me so that his erection pressed just where I needed it to.

His fingers found the hem of my skirt and slid beneath. I gasped. He pulled out of the kiss, his face hovering over mine once again with just that thin layer of thick breath between us. His eyes fixed to mine as his hands crept up my thigh. Those dark eyes, so like a hawk's, challenged me once again, seeing if I would fight or flee. I could do nothing but pant in anticipation.

"How's it going back there?" Hawk asked.

Back there? Back where? It took me a moment to realize that he wasn't talking to me.

"These fucking Bugs have tiny nuts. It's taking me a minute."

My body stiffened at the sound of the other man's voice. Eagle, I think it was.

"Doesn't look like we'll be long here. She's fit to blow. Isn't that right, sweet meat?" Hawk's gaze met mine, another challenge.

My heart was pounding so loud it rang in my ears. The blood pumped through my veins like the fluid was running its own race. But it must've been pumping south and not north because I didn't demand Hawk let me down. I kept my legs spread around his hips as his fingers crept closer to my panties.

All of this was happening with us in close proximity to three other guys. One of which I know was definitely watching from the other side of the street. The other two I suspected were taking peeks while fixing my flat tire.

When I voiced no opposition, Hawk's fingers hit home base. His thumb ran over the seam of my panties. I let out something between a whimper and a sigh.

"Fuck, you're wet, sweet meat. Is that fore me?"

I grabbed his shoulders as I trembled. Off in the distance, I saw blinking lights; fireflies coming nearer and nearer. Crickets chirped. Leaves rustled on the light breeze.

Hawk slipped his thumb beneath the seam of my panties until he touched my hot flesh. "Aw fuck, baby. You're sticky. Did you come already? That feels like fuck-cum."

I didn't know what he was talking about? The sound of cicadas singing filled my ears.

"I need to taste that shit. Give me your hand."

Hawk grabbed my hand from his chest. He put it beneath my skirt. I felt the sticky heat of my cunt. He dragged my fingers through, back and forth.

My eyes widened at the contact. I'd never touched myself before. Had I known it would feel this amazing, I would've done it years ago.

Hawk took my hand away from my panties, out from underneath my skirt, and put my fingers in his mouth. He sucked with his eyes closed. His tongue made my cunt clench. I tightened my legs around his hips.

"How's she taste, Hawk? She really sweet?"

Hawk licked the pads of my fingers, down to my knuckles, all the way to the webbing between each appendage. "She tastes like a ripe berry that ain't never been plucked."

The clatter of metal rang through the air again. "A virgin?"

"If I put my fingers deep inside you, Ellie, will I break your hymen?" Hawk asked. "Would you bleed for me, baby?"

I couldn't answer. I could only move my hips. The fireflies got closer. The cicadas sang louder.

Let them illuminate me. Let them tell the world what was happening on this block. I wanted Hawk to put his fingers inside me, and I didn't care who saw.

Hawk rubbed his thumb up and down the length of my cunt. I felt his fingernail scratching at my soft skin, like he was scratching an itch. I was itching, aching for him.

He alternated between dragging his nail down over my clit and onto the underside of my fleshy right labia. On the way back up on the left side, he'd run the rough pad of his thumb upwards.

"You're hairy, baby. You need to shave, that way you'll feel everything I can do to you."

Beneath my skirt, he spread my cunt lips wide. He made wide circles over the fleshy skin. His fingers had to be soaking by now. I felt my wetness trickling down my thighs. I heard myself between the layers of fabric. It was a cross between a slurping sound and a sucking sound.

Hawk pressed the length of his fingers against my cunt. The tips faced downward, right at my entrance. But he didn't venture inside. I moved my hips trying to angle him in.

He only chuckled in my ear and tsked. "That wasn't part of the deal."

Neither was him sticking his fingers in my cunt in front of an audience, but I'd made wiggle room for him. I wiggled against him now.

"Aw, let her have it, Hawk. She's begging for it."

I looked over to see the blond-headed Crow leaning over the trunk of the car, wrench in hand.

"Finish the fucking tire and let me handle this," Hawk growled.

There was no bite to Hawk's words. He barely spared Crow a glance. Hell, I barely spared Crow a glance. My attention zeroed back in on what was going on beneath my knee-length skirt.

Hawk took his pointer and middle finger and scissored my folds together, squeezing and pulling the two pieces of flesh. Then he took his thumb, and like a windshield wiper, he swatted at my clitoris. Back and forth, and back and forth.

My body shook. I felt like a cicada about to shed its skin. I felt like I was leaving behind my old body and being reborn into something new and beautiful. All my senses felt heightened. I felt the car move. I heard footsteps. I heard other breaths aside from mine and Hawk's.

The other two, Eagle and Crow, had finished with the tire and came to lean on the side of the car. They couldn't see my cunt because my skirt covered Hawk's hands. They weren't even looking down south. They both watched my face with fierce concentration. The rapt audience made my heart pound harder, the blood race faster.

"Fuck, she's close," said Crow.

"She's gonna come all over your hand," said Eagle. "She still got her panties on?"

"Yeah," Hawk grinned. "I got you, E."

Hawk ran his thumb in a clock-like pattern. Every time he got to my entrance he pushed a little deeper. With his other hand, he held my hips firm so I couldn't impale myself on him like I so desperately wanted to do. It was driving me mad.

"You're gonna gush your juices all over the place," said Hawk. "Aren't you, sweet meat?"

He went faster and faster. Around and around.

Then he'd stop the clock-like motion and start up the windshield wiping with his thumb.

"You want me inside you, don't you, sweet meat? You want my cock buried deep in your cunt?"

I turned away from Hawk and bit the inside of my elbow. Eagle and Crow had taken up sentry on either side of Hawk and I, but they kept their distance.

"She's tight isn't she? Tight, sweet, virgin meat." In my peripheral vision, I saw Crow bounce on his feet like a kid.

"Stop fucking around, Hawk," said Eagle. "Let the girl blow."

Eagle was my new hero. I turned to him in gratitude. He winked at me. But Hawk stole my attention back.

Hawk ran his fingers, light and fast, over my clitoris. I frowned in frustration. I wanted a hard, firm touch. But what did I know? His light flicks set off an earthquake inside of me. My body jerked, breaking free of my old skin.

I cried out at the first crack. My skin splintered. My body broke free. My eyes squeezed closed, shutting out the light of the fireflies. The sound of my cries drowned out the cricket's song.

And then all was silent. The flashing lights stopped. The streetlight blinked out. Not even the humming buzz of electricity coursed through the metal structure.

Hawk held me as I shook. Then slowly, he let my legs go and put me back on the ground. But as he put my legs down, he reached under my skirt one more time.

I was certain I couldn't take another earth shattering orgasm, but I didn't protest. He grabbed the elastic of my panties, and pulled down.

SIX

Hawk lifted my feet one at a time to relieve me of my panties. They were simple white cotton. I'd bought them in an eight-pack package from Target. Part of me was embarrassed that they weren't lace or a thong like I'd glimpsed some of the other girls wearing at the street racing party. But Hawk didn't appear to mind.

He straightened, holding the panties up to his nose. I felt mortified. Even without the light I could see the soaking wet crotch area as compared to the dry, starched top of the underwear.

Hawk waved the panties in the air, twirling them on his finger in front of Eagle. Eagle reached out and snatched the panties from Hawk's grasp.

Eagle put his nose in the crotch. With his eyes on me, he took a deep, open-mouthed inhale. His eyes shuttered closed in ecstasy.

When they reopened, they immediately found me. He turned the panties inside out. There was an evident fluid stain on the crotch area. Eagle stretched out his tongue and licked the length of the crotch area.

I pressed my knees together once more. My upper thighs slid off one another from the wetness that appeared watching Eagle tonguing my ruined underwear.

"Sweet as fucking berries." Eagle tucked the panties inside his back jeans pocket. Then he reached his hand out towards me.

I stared at his big, dark, claw-like hand for ten full seconds before setting my hand into motion. With my palm outstretched, Eagle dropped my car keys into my hand. I was so weak from my orgasm that the key chain nearly toppled me over.

Eagle reached past me and opened my car door. "She's all fixed up. You'll need to get a new spare in case something like this happens again."

I held onto my car door as I watched Eagle and Crow head back across the street towards their cars.

The two of them joined the other member of their crew who still stood in the same relaxed stance, still watching me. With their backs turned I read the wording on the back of Eagle and Crow's matching leather jackets.

Watchers Crew, it read.

I looked away from them to see that Hawk still stood before me. He regarded my face as an artist would a painting, as a chef would a new dish. He watched me like I would observe a new specimen of insect that I was about to dissect, trying to uncover how its systems worked.

Hawk reached out his hand. It didn't take me ten seconds to reach mine back to him. My hand was engulfed by his. He handed me into my car.

I didn't know what to say. "Thank you," I tried.

As soon as the words were out of my mouth I wished I could take them back.

Thank you for fixing my tire and not charging me an arm and a leg like any other mechanic would do.

Thank you for getting me off in the middle of the street while your boys watched.

Thank you for the mind-altering, paradigm shifting experience I might never recover from.

It didn't matter. I would not be seeing him or any of them again in this lifetime. I would head out of this neighborhood, back to my old life. My easy life that was all planned out.

"Looks like you're due for a tune up soon," he said. "You should come by our shop. We'll take care of you."

Hawk handed me a card with the address of his shop on it. "Same payment plan," he winked.

He put his thumb in his mouth and sucked it hard, making a loud popping sound when he pulled it out. "See you around, sweet meat." He winked and headed across the street.

Hawk ducked into his car. The other boys followed suit. With a roar of their engines they tore down the street.

I watched the fading taillights as they disappeared down the dark street. The street light above me turned on full bright once more. It stayed bright while I toyed with the business card Hawk had given me. The light blinked out again, casting me into the darkness of night. I placed the card in the cup holder so I wouldn't lose it in the dark.

Inside my car, I grabbed my owner's manual to put it back in the dash. Before I put it away, I flipped it over to the scheduled maintenance page. It read that a tune up should happen every 10,000 miles. I looked over at the odometer. I'd barely reached 4,000 miles.

SEVEN

I pulled open the top cover of the hive. As I did, the vibrations from the workers inside became louder. Their singing pinged through my entire body. Peering inside I saw that the hive was buzzing with activity. A healthy queen lay in the center, surrounded by her drones. The male bees lined up around her, waiting attentively, hoping to be chosen for the next round of copulation.

The queen took flight. Drones flanked her, trying desperately to keep up, to get ahead, so they might be chosen to enter the queen. Finally one gained the advantage. He mounted the queen from behind, aligning his penis with the queen. The copulation took less than a minute. I couldn't see any thrusting, but that didn't stop my imagination. Especially as I watched the other drones try to keep up, eager for a chance of their own.

I looked away from the mating queen and her drones to the enclosed garden where the wooden hive was set up. In the manmade garden, the female workers set about their daily tasks of visiting with the flowers. The worker bees' bodies were all no bigger than my thumb, their wings the size of my fingernail. But beating at a speed of 200 beats per second, their wings sent a strong vibration that made the bees take flight. I watched their wings flick fast, so fast the motion blurred. I heard the buzzing in my ears. I felt it go through me.

It started in my head, clouding my judgment.

Then I felt it sting my lips until they were swollen.

My nipples tightened as though they were touched with pinpricks, or little crawlers.

My belly trembled as the vibrations went lower, and lower. Remembering his finger flicking back and forth like a wing beating at my clit-

"Ellie,"

I jerked to consciousness and my clipboard clattered to the floor. I looked at Shakira who stood in the doorway of the greenhouse classroom.

"Hey sis, I know we're supposed to meet today,

but I wanted to let you know that something came up and I've gotta bail."

It had been two days since I'd seen Shakira. Two days since the street race. Two days since a man stuck his hands down my panties and made me take flight while his buddies flanked him and watched with admiration and eagerness.

I closed the lid and stepped out of the enclosure. My hands shook even though I couldn't hear or feel the buzzing of the hive any longer.

"That's okay," I said to Shakira.

She waved and made to back out of the classroom door.

"You headed off to another street race?" I asked.

Shakira narrowed her eyes at me.

It belatedly dawned on me that street racing was illegal and probably not something I should broadcast.

"Sorry," I said, though we were alone in the classroom.

"No, I'm not headed to a street race at ten in the morning. I've gotta work on my English Lit final. Jane Austen's a bitch."

I nodded in agreement, even though I owned the Austen compendium in hardback and ebook.

"If I have to read another story about some poor,

prissy, white girl falling over a rich, alpha lord I'm gonna slit my wrists. You feel me, sis?"

"Oh, yeah. I do. I feel you. No English lords for you... So, you like Asian men?"

Shakira studied me. My cheeks heated under her perusal. There was something knowing in the way she regarded me, like she saw right through me.

Well, of course she saw right through me. That segue into trying to get more information about the Watchers Crew had been weak. But she couldn't tell what I was thinking. She didn't know what happened that night.

Unless the boys told her. They probably had. They'd probably told everybody. They may have even taken pictures. Guys did that these days, and unsuspecting girls ended up on college tramp websites in lewd sexual positions and situations. They could've done that to me. Hawk had sent me outside of my body with his tongue in my mouth and his fingers inside me. I bet I looked like a tramp.

I wished I could see those pictures -if there were any. I wanted to have a memory of that night captured in print or pixels so that I could take it out, and look at it, and remember that feeling of euphoria.

When I shook off my haze of memory, I saw

Shakira smiling sadly at me. She shook her head from the left to the right. The look she gave me was one a mother would give to her teen daughter who thought she knew it all.

"Look, sis, you've been real helpful with biology. So, let me give you some life advice of my own. Stay away from the Watchers Crew. Those boys eat little girls like you up for breakfast. Which might feel really good in the morning, but then they spit you out by lunchtime." She turned and left.

I shoved my notes into my bag and headed out the building to my car. I caught my reflection in the glass doors as I went out. I looked the same as a few nights ago. I had on another knee length skirt, a blouse, and flats. I looked like I was going to a church brunch.

Shakira was right. I'd had that one experience. It should be enough to last a lifetime. If I were a smart girl, I shouldn't go back for more.

I came up to my car and climbed inside the driver's side door. Hawk had told me I was due for a tune up soon. I'd only had my Bug for six months. I was meticulous about the maintenance. I'd had the oil changed just last month. The scheduled maintenance wasn't for another 5,000 miles.

Hawk charged me two kisses to fix my tire. One

kiss on the mouth and another inside my panties while three guys watched. He'd said it would cost the same to get my tune up; a tune up I didn't need for months, maybe even a year.

A year seemed so far away. I'd be away from this place in a year. Jerry and I had talked about moving up north for him to go to grad school. There were a few job opportunities available for me there as well. Once Jerry and I were together, we'd likely fall into more traditional roles where he handled the car maintenance. I'd probably never have to get my oil changed myself again. I'd likely never go in for a tune up in my life.

Maybe I should go for this one. Just so I understood what would be done to my car once Jerry took over the scheduled maintenance. My cotton panties dampened at the thought of more kisses.

I leaned against the driver's seat and shook myself. What had gotten into me? Up until two days ago I'd barely spent time at second base with my boyfriend of a year. The same boyfriend who I'd agreed to go on a weekend trip with in just a few days. We'd undoubtedly be having sex for the first time. I'd planned to have my first time with Jerry for months now. It was finally about to happen and I was having wet dreams about kissing a man who I didn't even know.

I looked at the card that Hawk had given me. It sat in my cup holder. Just the sight of that small piece of paper made me rub my legs together. The name in gothic letters, *Watchers Crew Auto and Body*, made my heart pound just like when they were all watching me get fingered straight into bliss.

My phone rang causing me to drop the card. Jerry's face popped up on the caller ID. I stared at his face while the phone continued to ring. Jerry wasn't unattractive. He looked like the math major he was, the accountant he was destined to become.

Jerry had kissed me plenty of times. The sight of his face didn't kick up my heartbeat like that piece of paper sitting in my cup holder. Jerry had never put his hands down my panties either. Did I want Jerry to put his hands down my panties?

I hit the Accept button.

"Hey Jer."

"Jer?"

Jerry was short for Jeremiah. I noticed during the holidays when I spent time with him and his family I was the only person who called him that. He corrected everyone else with the use of his full name.

I'd thought it was a pet name, only for me to call him. It never occurred to me that he might not like it.

"Sorry," I said. "What's up? I thought you were in class."

"On a break. Just wanted to check in about this weekend. I was wondering if you'd mind us taking your car? I've gotta put mine in the shop and it's not going to be repaired in time."

"Sure, that's no problem. We can take my car."

"You're up to date on all your scheduled maintenance?"

I was about to answer when he huffed a laugh.

"What am I saying? Of course you are. You're so responsible. It's one of the things I like about you, Eleanor."

That was me, Eleanor Russell. Smart, dependable, reliable, good girl.

"Yeah," I said. "Well, I was just thinking about taking my car into the shop for a tune up. Just to be safe."

"Sounds good. Hey, I gotta get back to class. I can't wait to see you this weekend."

"Yeah. Me too."

He disconnected.

I put the key in the ignition and headed across town.

EIGHT

I pulled up twenty minutes later to Watchers Auto and Body. It was in a rough side of town, not too far from the race site. There were no trashcans on the street out in front of garages. Instead, a set of large green dumpsters sat at the end of the cul-de-sac I came across. Numerous cars lined driveways, many which sat on cement blocks instead of wheels.

Where I came from there was a clear division of where you lived and where you worked. Not so in this part of town. On the opposite side of the main street it looked as though I'd stepped into an industrial zone. Body shops, hardware stores, mechanic's signs for foreign and domestic cars beamed bright under the sun's glare.

I pulled up and parked on the street outside

Watchers Auto and Body. The corrugated, metal door to the garage was pulled down closed. I went up to the entrance and crossed the threshold.

No one stood behind the service counter. The waiting chairs lined up against the wall were all empty. I heard music blaring deeper into the shop. I ventured further and came onto the work floor.

I saw a thick pair of booted legs underneath a car. Then I saw two large figures standing in a doorway. I recognized the blond locks of Crow leaning against the doorjamb. The dark-haired male next to him was the silent watcher from the other night, the Asian whose name I still had yet to catch.

The Asian guy turned as though he heard me approach over the blaring music. His eyes looked me up and down, slowly. I felt like wherever his eyes landed on me was a caress. He made no move to come closer. He said nothing. He leaned his body against the opposite doorjamb. With his massive body no longer obstructing my view, I saw into the room.

A woman was splayed over a desk. Her naked ass was in the air. Her hands gripped the corners of the desk. Her head was reared back in ecstasy. She had the hugest open-mouthed grin on her face. High-pitched grunts came through her open mouth as her body jerked rhythmically. Then I saw what made her body jerk rhythmically, what put that grin on her face.

It was Hawk.

He had the woman's hair wrapped around his huge paw. The other hand gripped her ass as he pummeled his bare hips into her from behind. His chest was bare. His cargo pants fell open at his hips. I saw a dark patch of curls that surrounded his huge cock. His length appeared and disappeared inside the woman's bared cunt. I saw a purple piece of elastic at the base of his penis.

"Take it," he rammed into her. "You're a dirty, little whore aren't you, Mrs. Pettigrew."

"Yes. I. Am." Mrs. Pettigrew said in time with Hawk's brutal thrusts. "I'm a filthy slut who loves your cock in my pussy."

"What would your husband say if he knew I was fucking this pretty pussy?" Hawk slapped her ass.

The crack made me jump.

"Maybe, I should tell him?" Hawk taunted.

"No. Please." The please was a sigh of such pleasure that I wondered if Mrs. Pettigrew wanted her husband to find out. If she wished her husband was the one standing in the doorway instead of Hawk's crew.

"You don't want me to tell him? Then suck my dick." Hawk pulled himself from behind her and turned her around. He took her face in both hands and impaled her face on his dick.

Mrs. Pettigrew swallowed him until her nose met his pubic hairs. I could hear her gurgling. Hawk was massive. There was no way he fit comfortably into her angular cheeks. In fact, I saw the imprint of his bulbous cockhead poking the side of her cheek.

She didn't struggle. She put her hands on the base of his cock, stroking it up and down as she sucked on his thick, round head.

Hawk slapped her hands away. "There you go again, cheating. Just like the dirty, fucking whore you are. Move your hands away. Take my whole dick."

He grabbed her chin. She winced. But looking further, I could tell that was not a wince of pain, her face slackened with pure pleasure.

"Put your hand on my dick again without my permission and I'll call your husband; tell him what a cheating, little bitch you are."

Mrs. Pettigrew put her hands behind her back and opened her mouth wide. Hawk stuffed his dick all the way down her throat again. There was no poking into the side of her cheek. He pumped his hips down into her mouth, his dick never withdrawing more than halfway out of her mouth. She sounded like she was gargling mouthwash.

He pumped fast and hard for a good thirty seconds. When he withdrew to the tip, Mrs. Pettigrew took a deep breath. Before she had completely exhaled, Hawk stuffed his dick in her mouth again and repeated the process. She slobbered and drooled down his massive dick. The slobber landed on her pert breasts.

Mrs. Pettigrew put her hands between her legs and found her clit. She began that windshield wiper motion that I'd recently come to know.

Hawk gave her hair a tug. "Get your fucking hands off your clit. Did I say you could come? Greedy little, bitch. Think you can come before me?"

He slowed his motions, withdrawing all but the tip of his dick from her mouth, and then stuffing himself into her face until her lips touched his balls. He held her there. She squirmed and gurgled but she didn't struggle. When he pulled out moments later she whimpered and tried to follow him. He pumped his cock with his hand once, twice, and came all over her face. His eyes wide, his grin wider.

That's when he looked up and saw me. His smile

went even wider as he scanned down my body. He jerked a third time, this time a few droplets spilled into her mouth.

Mrs. Pettigrew lapped the droplets up like she'd been in a desert and his semen was the first drops of water she'd received in days. After the last drop, she suckled at his cockhead. Hawk broke his gaze from mine and looked back down at her. I was finally able to look away.

I'd watched the complete sex act without an ounce of shame. But when he caught me staring at him I felt completely humiliated.

What was I thinking coming here? Shakira had tried to warn me. I'd been breakfast a couple of days ago and they'd already moved on. It was lunchtime.

I turned to go but crashed into a big, black chest.

NINE

"Hey, sweet meat," Eagle said.

I got the impression he'd been standing behind me for a long time, watching me watch Hawk. Just like the Asian guy who'd moved over to be sure I'd see what was going on in the room.

"I'm sorry," I said to his chest. I couldn't meet his eyes. "I shouldn't have come. I'll go."

"I like that you came."

He grinned when he said it. I was smart enough to know he'd meant it as a double entendre.

"Did you need me to look at your car?" Eagle asked.

"I... I..."

"Come on." He put his hand on the small of my

back and gave me a gentle shove. "Let's pop the hood. See what's going on under there."

My focus was on the large hand at the small of my back and how good that pressure felt there after I'd watched another woman get what I'd come for. With that hand easing the pressure I hadn't realized had built up in my core, I let him guide me back out into the main workroom.

"I'm sorry we missed you coming in," Eagle said. "We were working on another job."

"Yeah, I saw. Look, I don't mean to bother you guys-"

"You're no bother at all, sweet meat. Like I said, I'm glad you came." He grinned at me. "I was worried about you after we let you go the other night. Didn't know if you knew your way out. We should've waited to make sure you got home safe. That was thoughtless of us."

"I got home okay."

"And now you're here." His thumb made that windshield wiper motion on my hip.

"I am. But the scheduled maintenance on my car isn't for another 5,000 miles. I really don't need the work done."

Eagle's thumb continued the back and forth hypnotic motion. My clit swelled in time to its tick tock. His four other fingers dug into the small of my back. "Do you want it?"

I swallowed and tried to focus on the words coming out of his mouth. The words he said, not what he might have meant.

"Do you want me to look under your hood?" he clarified slowly.

His other hand rose to the other side of my hip, mimicking the same motion. All the blood in my brain rushed south.

I nodded. "Yeah, I want you to look under my hood."

"Good." Eagle's smile was wicked, a wolf taking off his sheep's mask.

He pulled his hands away and crossed them over his massive chest. "You'll have to pay up front."

The blood rushing back up to my head gave me a brain freeze as I snapped out of his seductive trance to witness the businessman standing before me. My purse was slung over my shoulder. I reached over to unzip it.

Eagle stayed my hand before I could pull out my wallet. "I believe Hawk already explained our payment plan to you."

I swallowed. "You want a kiss?" My head was already tilting up to meet his lips.

Eagle frowned as though I'd offered him a used piece of chewing gum. "I'm not interested in sticking my tongue in your mouth, sweet meat. Give me your panties."

"You want my panties?"

"For starters. And then I'm going to part those pretty thighs of yours, spread your pussy lips, stick my tongue in your cunt, and make you come so hard you cry. After that, I'll take a look at your car. Does that sound like a fair deal, sweet meat?"

Crow and the Asian one came out into the workroom. They leaned against the wall as though deciding whether to look my way or back in the other room. I heard Mrs. Pettigrew climaxing amidst loud thumps of the desk. Crow looked over his shoulder and back into the room.

Now, I'm not a competitive person by nature. But suddenly I wanted -no, needed- all of their attention on no one else but me.

"Give me your car keys."

I did as Eagle said and handed over my keys. He disappeared out the door. Not five minutes later, he pulled my car onto the work floor and shut the metal gates behind him. I was shut in, trapped, with these men who had every intention of fucking me. My heart was pounding, but the last thing I wanted to do was run away.

Eagle's offer buzzed around in my head. But my attention was focused on the other two men I could see on the other side of the room, and the one I couldn't. More than embarrassment, I felt jealous that that woman was getting the treatment I had come here hoping for.

For the past couple of days I'd been dreaming of Hawk putting his hands down my panties. Hawk licking his fingers and then wanting more and putting his face between my legs. That wouldn't be enough for him, and he'd finally have to fuck me.

I hated that it was her that his dick was in and not me. But, even more, I hated that all their attention was on someone other than me. So, I did the only thing I could.

When Eagle hopped out of my car, I took my panties off and handed them to him. Crow and the Asian one came into the room and sat down on a workbench in front of my car.

Eagle did the same thing he'd done that first night. He turned my panties inside out and buried his nose in the crotch. He didn't lick this time. Instead, he tossed them over to Crow who caught them mid air.

"Fucking, sweet," said Crow who did lick the crotch area. "Take a hit, Owl."

Owl, formerly known as the Asian one, took my panties without a word. I saw the dampness from where I stood before Eagle. Owl wrung the crotch fabric around his fingers. He twisted until a single drip of my honey landed on his tongue.

It was just a drop, but my mind went back to my bees. Each honeybee only produces one-twelfth a teaspoon of honey in its entire lifetime. There was more than that coming out of me now watching Owl lick the crotch of my panties.

Hawk walked out of his office just then with Mrs. Pettigrew on his arm. He spoke to her quietly, no longer shouting at her or calling her filthy names. I watched him lead her to the door. She reached up to tug his head down, but he only offered her his cheek. Mrs. Pettigrew took what she could get and smacked her red lips against Hawk's cheek.

Before she turned out the door, she glanced over at me. I saw her massive chest of fake boobs rise and fall. She didn't exactly wink at me. She raised her eyebrows as though to say, "Have fun," and then she left.

Hawk turned and his eyes surveyed the room. I watched him take in Crow and Owl passing my panties back and forth. I watched him take in Eagle who stood before me.

"Hey Ellie," Hawk said. "You came in for some servicing?"

"Yeah," my voice wobbled. "Like you said, my scheduled maintenance is coming up soon."

"Is that so?" He gave me that mischievous grin.

It was another challenge. We both knew what the mileage on my odometer read. We both knew I wasn't due for any maintenance for months.

"Yeah, that's so," I said. "I really like my car. I want to give it the best care possible."

Hawk grinned wider. I'd passed this test.

"Eagle said he'd take care of me."

Hawk turned to Eagle, his grin faltering.

The side of Eagle's mouth ticked up in a challenge of his own. "Yeah, I'm gonna take care of her."

They were like two birds of prey circling a juicy chunk of helpless meat.

After a brief stand off, Hawk backed off. He smiled and clapped Eagle on the back. "You gonna give her some head?"

"For starters," Eagle drawled.

There was another tense silence. I saw Hawk's fingers clench and release Eagle's shoulders. Then he released the man, his grin back in check. Hawk leaned into me. "Eagle's fairly decent at giving girls head. I watched him make a girl pass out once."

"Twice," Eagle corrected.

Hawk ignored Eagle. He planted a chaste kiss on my forehead. "I'm glad you came by, Ellie." He reached down and pulled up my skirt. He looked back at me, grinning. "And you shaved."

I'd done so the morning after he'd put his fingers down my panties. I'd had to. All the hair between my legs felt like it was weighing me down after that encounter. So I got rid of it, and I felt instantly free. Now, seeing his pleased look, I was glad I'd done it.

Hawk's eyes were bright with excitement. "It's gonna be even better, sweet meat. You'll see." He walked over to the workbench and took a seat. He grabbed my panties from Owl, balled them up in his hand and put them against his nose.

I stood there in a room full of strong, powerful men who could have their way with me. But I wasn't the least bit afraid. Drones, male bees, have no stinger. Their only purpose in life is to mate the queen. I felt a hum of energy coming off all these guys as they trained their eyes on me, waiting for me to open for them, to take flight so they could chase me down and be the first to mount me.

TEN

"Take off your shoes, sweet meat," said Eagle. "I don't want you to mess up your cute, little paint job."

I tore my eyes away from Hawk and my panties, and slipped off my flats. Eagle hefted me up onto the hood of my car. My bare ass met with cool metal.

"Spread those pretty, thighs for me."

There were four sets of eyes on me. Their eagerly patient facades emboldened me. I focused on the dark set of eyes before me. This is what I'd come here for. Maybe not the guy I'd come here for. But Eagle was just as big as Hawk. Just as handsome. Just as dangerous.

They were the same, but different. First, there were the obvious differences. Hawk was tan with tufts of dark hair. Eagle was brown with a bald head.

Both males were big, intimidating men. Hawk appeared more mischievous with his intimidation, as though he dared you to cross him. Eagle had a wariness about him, like he didn't want to be crossed, didn't want to be tried, but he would put anyone down who crossed the line.

I opened my legs for Eagle's brown gaze. He raised my hips up and rolled my skirt past my butt, up to my waist. I felt metal meet my ass. I heard a chorus of groans.

"Look at that fucking, pink pussy."

"Virgin pussy."

"God damn, I love an untouched cunt."

Eagle pushed my thighs wider. I realized it was so that the others could see my pretty, pink pussy better. He placed one hand on my belly to hold me still. I hadn't realized I was shivering. His eyes locked on mine as he licked his lips. Then he struck my cunt, like a match on flint. I collapsed back onto the hood of the car.

He licked at me; slow licks with achingly long seconds of space in between each one. It reminded me of summer time, eating an ice cream cone in the blazing heat. You started at the top, but then inevitably the cream would heat and trickle down the side. You'd have to take long licks from the bottom of the cone up to the top. Then try again to get to the top, only to have another trickle drop down the other side of the cone. That was Eagle's process of eating out my warm, dripping pussy.

I tried to anticipate when the next strike would come, but there was no rhythm to his motions. I opened my eyes to look down instead of trying to anticipate, and I saw what he was doing. After each lick, he'd take a few seconds to savor the juices he'd collected on his tongue. I swear that made me gush more juices.

Eagle groaned as honey gushed out of me. For a moment, he stopped his furtive licks and just stared. Then his lips surrounded my clit. He pulled like he was taking a long drag of a cigarette. He puckered his lips and sucked, then relaxed them and blew.

Suck and blow, suck and blow.

I lost all propriety and gyrated my hips to the beat of his tongue. I felt a tightening in my core. Eagle must've felt it too because he snuffed out his machinations. It didn't cool the flame within me. I whimpered in frustration. Eagle looked up at me with that wary expression that warned me not to cross him. Or else.

Thoroughly chastised, I settled my hips down and waited for him to make his next move.

"Look at how fucking wet she is. She's a fucking faucet."

I was coming to recognize Crow's voice, coming to pair it with the wide-eyed enthusiasm of an adolescent boy.

I recognized Hawk's deep, rumble of wordless agreement.

I sensed Owl's silent eyes watching me.

It was as though I could scent each one of them out. Many insects knew each other by scent, bees especially. Their olfactory abilities enabled them to communicate with one another, find food, identify the differences between flowers, and to recognize their kin.

Eagle inserted a finger inside me. "Fuck me, she's tight."

"I told you so," said Hawk.

"Ain't nobody ever try to get in this sweet pussy before?" Eagle asked. "Never took it out for a test drive?"

I think I shook my head *no* in answer to Eagle's question. My head was definitely shaking from the left to the right and then back again at the sweet agony his finger created inside me. He inserted another finger and my knees knocked together.

Eagle patiently pried them apart. His eyes

warned me not to do it again. I let my knees fall open wide for him.

Inside me, I felt him crook those two fingers as though he were telling me to come here. He stroked up and down. At first gently. The sensation wasn't as pleasant as when he just had one finger pointing upwards inside me. Then he sped up his motions.

I felt heat building inside me. The pressure inside me felt like I was a full well and he was opening a damn somewhere deep inside me. As he sped his come-hither fingers up and down in a single spot, I felt the damn break and the waters it held rushed into the spot in me that was already full and brimming.

But I wasn't coming.

Not like I had with Hawk.

It felt like I had jumped past that tension-snapping type of orgasm and I was approaching another deeper level. I was almost there, almost to the level. My hips jerked with Eagle's motions. I panted. I needed something to push me through the barrier, but I didn't know what?

Eagle winked at me as though he knew exactly what was going on inside me. He lent down with a wicked grin that made my belly clench. He dipped his head, and I felt his tongue on my clit as his fingers continued the come-hither motion inside me. All it took was a few strokes of his tongue, as though his tongue was the lock turning the key inside me. The doors deep inside me opened, and all of heaven and hell broke loose.

As the gates inside me crashed open, in my periphery I saw Crow and Owl's mouths part, eyes rapt on me. I found Hawk in my immediate eye line. His eyes were wide, taking it all in. His mouth was tight with tension as though he'd held his breath as the pressure mounted inside me.

I had been holding my breath too as the orgasm climbed higher and higher. It was like taking a running leap off a diving board. I took in a big breath of air when I went airborne, and then held it until I hit the water.

I sailed through the gates on a tidal wave and then I hit the water, hard. My breath gushed out of me on a guttural moan. My eyes never left Hawk's. He sighed, too, at the impact of my release. Neither of us blinked as I trembled and shook.

Hawk was right. I came so hard I thought I would pass out. I felt the flood that overran the well inside of me gush out and down my thighs. I felt the wetness on my butt.

Eagle removed his fingers. He grabbed both of

my thighs and pulled my hips to his face. He slurped up all the stickiness between my legs, calling down more and licking that up too until I was nearly clean and dry.

My body collapsed back on the hood of my car. The bump on the hood created an arch in my back that pushed my hips up. I felt Eagle stand between my legs. I felt clothing rustle between my thighs.

"What the fuck do you think you're doing?" I recognized Hawk's voice. There was no mischief in his tone. He sounded pissed.

I rose up on my elbows and peered up. Eagle had unzipped his pants and had his penis out in his hand, aimed at my still throbbing core.

"What does it look like? I'm going to fuck her."

Hawk shoved Eagle back from my entrance. "You know the rules, E. I always get the first taste of any new tail."

"You just fucked Mrs. Pettigrew."

"Watching Ellie come got me hard again," Hawk said. "I'm going to fuck her first."

Eagle's jaw looked as hard as flint. His hand flexed around his penis. Hawk's nose flared with aggression. I feared they'd come to blows right before my exposed, intimate flesh.

"At least go wash your fucking dick," Eagle growled.

Hawk cocked his head in a birdlike motion of confusion.

"Don't be disrespectful to Ellie," Eagle said. "You got another woman's cunt juices all over you. You planning to put your dirty dick in her sweet meat?"

Hawk considered this, and then nodded. "Hold that thought, sweet meat. I'll be right back." He dashed off.

Eagle scowled after him, tucking his penis back into his pants. "Greedy ass, mother fucker."

Crow got up from his seat and came over. "Hey, Ellie. You think I could have a little taste before Hawk gets back?"

I blinked. Crow's eyes weren't on my exposed cunt. They were on my covered breasts.

"I gotta thing for pink tits," he said. "I bet yours are rosy."

The thing I was coming to notice about Crow was that his gleeful smile was infectious. I relaxed back down onto the hood with a matching smile on my face. I lifted a shaky hand to my blouse, but Crow stopped me.

"Nah, sweet meat. I got it." He opened my shirt, one button at a time.

When my shirt was completely open, he took off my bra one handed. Crow looked like he was ready to cry at the sight of my bare breasts. He bent down slowly. I saw his tongue peek out. He delicately gave one nipple a lick. Then he brought the breast fully into his mouth.

Crow did the same pull and blow motion that Eagle had used on my cunt. It didn't matter where that rhythm was played on my body. It had the same effect. I felt another floodgate open from somewhere deep inside me, ready to let loose another store of juices.

"Holy fuck," said Crow. "I think she'd fuck-cum just from me sucking her tits."

"You can suck them after I'm done. Move out of the way." Hawk was back.

Eagle and Crow both took a seat on the bench next to the ever quiet, ever-watchful Owl.

Hawk took off his shirt. Then he slowly unbuttoned his pants. "You want it, Ellie?"

His massive erection sprang free. I lost my breath, and my nerve, at the sight of it.

"You gotta ask for it."

I nodded. "I do. I want it, Hawk." He came up between my legs and I winced.

"Don't worry, sweet meat." He rolled on a condom one handed. "With as much fucking as we do, we always strap up."

"That's not what I'm worried about."

Hawk followed the trajectory of my gaze. He looked up and grinned. "You worried that it won't fit?"

I nodded.

He ran his finger over my lips. "Don't worry about that, baby. I can tell you it won't fit. But we're gonna work it until it does."

He put his fingers in me. His fingers were just as thick as Eagle's, but instead of reaching upwards, Hawk spread his fingers outwards.

"Yeah, Hawk," said Crow as he sat back on the couch. "Stretch that sweet, tight pussy."

Hawk removed his fingers and put the thick head of his penis at my core. Though he'd stretched me a second ago, it did little to prepare me for his girth. He spread my thighs wider and went a little deeper. I clutched at his back.

"Aw fuck," he growled. "Don't use your nails, sweet meat. Not unless you want it rough."

I thought about him pounding into Mrs. Pettigrew, slapping her ass, and shoving his penis down her throat. I'd been appalled and turned on at the same time. But I didn't want that. Not the rough sex, because thinking back on it, it had been so impersonal. I didn't want him calling me any names other than my own, or sweet meat. I didn't want him to slap my ass. I didn't want him to shove my face into the car's hood. I wanted him looking me in the eye, taking his time, telling me how good I felt, promising to make me feel good. All the things he was doing right now. I retracted my nails and held my breath as he stretched away my virginity.

"Breathe, Ellie." Hawk looked in my eyes and smiled down at me.

I did as he told me. He pushed further in.

"I know you want it, baby. I'm gonna give it to you. I'm gonna give it all to you. And I'm gonna feel that sweet meat come around me."

I felt my skin stretched to the breaking point. I felt at any minute I'd tear and we'd have to stop. I didn't want to stop. I willed my body to relax.

Hawk pushed in more. My eyes teared. My breath came so fast I was nearly hyperventilating. I felt invaded, and he wasn't even half way in. And then something in me snapped.

I felt that tight rope of tension I had when we'd

been out in the middle of the street last weekend. This time it didn't pull me in two different directions; it pulled me in every imaginable direction.

"Fuck," said Eagle. "She's coming, isn't she?"

"Again?" said Crow. "No fucking way."

Hawk's eyes opened wide as my body shook from the inside out. I felt myself fisting around him. My cunt clutched and released, clutched and released, and then he was pulled all the way inside of me.

With him covering more real estate, the orgasm kept going on and on. He lost control. He pumped into me. Not as hard as with Mrs. Pettigrew, but not as finessed as moments before.

"Look, she's gonna make him blow, man."

"Go, sweet meat. Take him the fuck down."

I watched as Hawk's big body crumbled around me. I felt his heart pounding into my chest. His breaths were harsh, fast, and shallow. He clutched me to him, so tightly I thought my bones might break.

He was all the way inside of me now. Hip to hip, chest-to-chest, forehead to forehead. I felt him in my belly, in my heart, in my soul. I felt in that moment I was his and he was mine. That we were joined inextricably together, and no one, and nothing could ever pull us apart.

Hawk pulled out of me.

There was awe on his face, all mischief gone. He looked at me in wonder, his face open and vulnerable. I felt a moment of fear at the sight of it. This big man who could crush me with his pinkie finger trembled over top of me. I knew he felt it too; that soul deep connection.

He planted a chaste kiss at my temple, then lower on my nose, he moved down to my mouth, but stopped. He hovered over my lips for half a second, but it felt like an eternity. I tilted my lips, eager to taste him. But he closed his mouth, shuttered his expression, and pulled off of me.

"You ready, E?" Hawk backed away from me. He still hadn't taken his eyes off me, but it didn't matter. They were shuttered now. The mischievous grin back. The challenge back. He waited to see if I'd protest.

Eagle rose from the bench. "You think she can handle it after that?"

Hawk smiled at me with something close to pride in his eyes. "Yeah, our little sweet meat can take it. She can take anything. Can't you, sweet meat?"

He didn't wait for me to answer. If he had waited he'd have heard me say I wanted no one but him. That I wanted him back inside my cunt and my mouth.

But Hawk backed away from me on shaky legs. I watched his hard ass disappear into his pants and then my view of him was obstructed by another thick, dark man who eyed me warily, daring me to tell him no.

ELEVEN

Eagle passed Hawk on his way to the bench. The two high fived, any tension from before gone.

Eagle unzipped his pants. "Can you handle it, sweet meat?"

I knew I should've said no. But a part of me didn't want to disappoint Hawk. So, I nodded.

Eagle grabbed a condom. He slid into my folds without preamble. His descent was easier, but he was thicker where Hawk was longer.

"Holy shit!"

I heard Hawk chuckling from the bench. "Yeah. I know, brother."

"Fuck," Eagle shut his eyes as he slid all the way in.

"Hold up. I gotta see this." Crow materialized

over my shoulder. "Dude that shit's poetry. Ebony and ivory."

Eagle set a slow rhythm. In, out. In, out, and around. In, out. In, out, and around.

"Make them bounce, E."

I assumed Crow meant my breasts since he hadn't taken his eyes off them since he'd come over to join us. Eagle, who had his eyes closed in ecstasy, ignored Crow and kept his slow rhythm that didn't cause my small breasts to jiggle much.

Crow took matters into his own hands. He reached out and ran his fingers over my right breast. I gasped.

Eagle opened one eye. "Crow, wait your fucking turn." Eagle thrust deep and closed his eyes again.

Crow ran his hand over the left nipple. I bucked.

"Crow!"

"I can't help it, man. They're like little rose buds." With two hands, Crow pinched both my nipples. That coupled with Eagle's wide girth filling me to capacity caused my body to seize.

This orgasm was at the thin line between pleasure and pain as my stretched cunt contracted around Eagle's thickness. It was like a jackhammer hitting solid metal. Both Eagle and I cried out. I felt his penis twitching, felt the tension in his muscles as he tried to hold onto his orgasm.

"She pull you under too?" Crow bounced on his feet like he had the other night.

"You fucking ass hole!" Eagle gave him a shove. "Get the fuck outta here."

Crow went back to the bench to a laughing Hawk and a grinning Owl.

Eagle was still hard inside of me. He withdrew and turned me over, placing my knees on either side of the hump in the bug's hood. He entered me from behind. He was no longer slow and in control. He pummeled into me like a piston. His hands played with my butt cheeks. He separated them, exposing my anus to the cool air. He rubbed me there with his thumb, in a circle motion.

At first I tensed at so intimate a touch. Then I remembered, I was fucking a virtual stranger in front of his three friends. This, after performing various other sex acts with two other guys, which included losing my virginity, oral sex, and breast play. I closed my eyes and enjoyed the new sensation.

After a while, I felt Eagle hitting that same spot he'd found with his fingers earlier. With each thrust of his hips, I felt the floodgates, which had never closed, opening impossibly wider. The pounding rhythm pushed a little fluid out each time. Before I knew it, I was full and bursting once more. To Crow's glee, I took Eagle down with me.

I expected Eagle to come with a roar like Hawk. But Eagle came quietly. He clutched me to him, opened his mouth wide and spilled into me.

"You're the fucking sweetest meat I've ever tasted, Ellie," he whispered in my ear before withdrawing from me.

Then I felt airborne. I opened my eyes to see thick, tan pecs and a corded neck. Hawk carried me away to the applause and catcalls of Crow. Owl looked on with a smile and a nod.

Hawk carried me to the back of the shop. We went into a bathroom that was nicer than what I'd expect for a mechanic's shop. He sat me on the corner of the sink. The cold tile was heaven against my throbbing core.

He ran the faucet and put a cloth underneath the water. After ringing the cloth of excess water, he cleaned me up. First my face, then my hands. Then on to my breasts, down to my belly. He put the cloth into the hot water before putting it onto my throbbing cunt. I closed my eyes and hissed at the contact.

I felt soft lips against my temple. "You did good,

sweet meat. You're gonna be fucking sore tomorrow."

I opened my eyes. "It was worth it."

I couldn't read his expression. His lips were parted, his eyes narrowed. His breath came out in a slow sigh of heat across my nose.

"Let's get you dressed," he said finally. "I'll drive you home. Eagle will have your car ready tomorrow night. Don't be surprised if he tricks it out after that performance."

Owl brought my bra and blouse to the bathroom door. He stayed and watched as Hawk dressed me. Hawk put on my bra and my blouse. I noticed my panties peeking out of his back pocket. He didn't offer them up.

I headed back out to the workroom behind Hawk. There was already a throbbing between my legs. Crow swooped me up in a bear hug. Looking over his shoulder, Owl nodded his head at me in something resembling a bow of respect.

Eagle blew me a kiss and licked his lips. Then he grabbed my panties from Hawk's back pocket. "I'll fix her up good for you, sweet meat."

"I know you will," I said. "Thank you, Eagle. Thanks, guys."

They all shuffled awkwardly under my gratitude

making a humming sound that sounded like a drone to me.

"Come on, Ellie," said Hawk. "Let's get you home."

"Have a good night guys." I turned and followed Hawk out. He handed me into his car. He reached over and buckled me into the seat belt. Then he got in on his side. I gave him my address, and we took off.

We were silent for a mile. I didn't know what to say. He didn't appear to need to fill the silence. He pulled out onto the highway. I opened my mouth to tell him he was going the wrong way when I noticed the speedometer climbing.

He reached 70. Then 80.

My heart pounded as I watched the street, the cars, the scenery whiz by. I felt the vibration of the wheels through the seat. I pressed my hips into the seat to get closer to the vibration. My breath kicked up.

He pushed it to 90. I pushed my legs together. The vibrations felt like they clocked over 200 beats a minute. I felt that at any minute we'd take flight.

I jumped when I felt his hand on my thigh.

I opened for him.

With no underwear on, Hawk pressed his

middle finger right up against my cunt. Aside from the wheel hitting the asphalt, I heard the slurping stickiness of my wetness. I heard my breath coming fast.

Hawk hit 100 miles per hour.

I strained against the seat belt to lift my hips and pushed my cunt into his fingers. I grabbed behind the headrest for leverage.

Hawk began a sawing motion with his fingers. I felt the leather of the seats dampen beneath my bare ass. My legs shook, and I went over. I cried out in the confines of the car as the blasted seat belt held me in place. I needed to get closer to Hawk and his wonderful fingers.

When I opened my eyes we were outside my dorm in the parking lot. Hawk cut the engine. He pushed his seat back. Then he reached over and yanked off my seat belt. He yanked me out of the seat. Up and over him I went until I was in his lap.

He worked to get his pants undone. I felt him shaking as he struggled with the condom. And then he was in me. There was no slow entry. There was no finesse. He pumped into me deep and hard and fast. My teeth rattled at his speed and power. I held onto the back of the driver's side headrest for dear life.

We were in the middle of the parking lot. The sun had set, but still we were parked under a street lamp. Anyone could walk by and see us.

I didn't care. I lifted my blouse so he could suckle my breasts. When his lips tugged on my nipple I felt another orgasm blooming inside me

"Fuck," he growled. "You gonna come again?" His voice was filled with incredulity.

I came with a helpless whimper.

He came with a deep growl.

His arms locked around me like a vice until we caught our breaths.

TWELVE

We sat like that for I don't know how long? Finally, Hawk pulled away. He ran his hand down the side of my face as though testing my skin for realness.

"I need to go," he said.

I tried to hop off him. He lifted my hips and placed me back in the passenger seat. Then he leaned his back against the driver's door and stared at me. He reached over and straightened my skirt. Then he turned and climbed out the door.

He came around to the passenger door and let me out. He took my hand and didn't let it go. I thought he'd say goodbye and leave me in the street. Instead, he asked which was my building.

He walked me to my dormitory. Walked me up

to my floor. Once there, we stood outside my door, facing each other.

"You got a roommate?" he asked.

"No," I said. "I'm a senior. Only freshmen have roommates. And then after your freshmen year it's by choice."

He looked at the door. Then he looked at me. I saw him wrestling with something.

"You wanna come in?" I asked.

Hawk shook his head. "I don't do sleepovers. I don't do the boyfriend-girlfriend thing. I don't do romance or handholding."

I wanted to remind him that he held my hand coming up to the building, and continued on up the stairs. Instead, I said, "I have a boyfriend. He goes to another school. We've been going out for a year, but we've never..."

"A year? And he never...?"

I shook my head. "I probably should've told you about him... you know before."

"Doesn't bother me. I don't believe in monogamy."

"Oh."

"But you do," he said. "Don't you, sweet meat? You believe in monogamy, being faithful, and all that shit. You probably feel guilty right now, like you cheated on him. You regret fucking us?"

"I…" I had believed in all that. Before Hawk put his hands down my panties. Now, the only thing I knew was, "I want you to fuck me again. Not tonight, of course. But some other day. Maybe?"

Hawk studied me again, weighing whatever was on his mind. Finally, he came out with it. "I'm having a party tomorrow night."

"Yeah?"

"Yeah." He reached out for the tail of my blouse and straightened it. "You should come." He grinned. "You're so good at it. You've come how many times today?"

"I don't know? I wasn't counting."

"Six, maybe?"

"Is that a lot?"

Hawk shrugged. "I read somewhere that over half of all women never come once in their lifetime."

My eyes widened.

"Yeah, it's tragic isn't it?"

"Well," I said. "I guess I'm good for years to come."

Hawk said nothing for a minute. Just stared at me. "I want you to come to my party, Ellie."

"Okay. I'll be there. But, I'll need a ride. You guys have my car."

My car was my pride and joy, and I'd just turned it over to these guys who I'd only known existed for less than three days.

"Oh, I'll give you a ride, sweet meat."

I got the joke and grinned along with him. "I'd like that. I'll come."

"Yes. You will." Hawk grinned, but then sobered. "Ellie, most girls make a big deal about their first time. I don't want you to do that. Think about it like getting your driver's license. It's like a permit for you to go anywhere with anyone."

I thought about that for a second. I'd had little qualms about fucking Eagle before or after I'd fucked Hawk. I was looking forward to fucking Crow, and curious about Owl. And then, there was Jerry this weekend...

"But don't go driving with anyone else for a while," Hawk said.

I blinked. "Okay," I agreed.

"Okay."

He leaned in and kissed my forehead, then my nose, he leaned down towards my lips. I assumed he wasn't going to kiss me. I didn't understand why not? He'd invaded my mouth the first night we met. But, to my surprise, he brushed his lips lightly over mine. If I'd moved a millimeter we'd be miles a part.

I held perfectly still. We stayed like that, lips just barely touching for I don't know how long. When he pulled away we both were panting.

Hawk looked at my door handle. Then shook his head. "We used you pretty good, sweet meat. You're going to be sore. Soak in a warm bath, but don't use soap. It'll just irritate that sweet pussy of yours."

"Okay."

"Okay," he mimicked with a smirk. "Sweet dreams, sweet meat."

And then he disappeared down the stairs.

I sighed, leaning against my door. I turned to open the door but noticed movement. Standing down the hall, gaping at me was Shakira.

Shakira who had warned me that guys like Hawk ate up little girls like me for breakfast and spit us out for lunch.

I shrugged my shoulders at her gaping expression. "I went over at lunchtime and he had me for dinner." I said before I went into my room and shut the door behind me.

THIRTEEN

I pushed the door closed with my butt and dropped my books and bag on the floor. It had been a long day. Every one in the lab was in a tizzy over the annual mayfly mating. It was that one day of the year when the insects rose from the lakes and streams. They had only one day, a few hours, to stretch their wings and take to the skies. One day to experience life and everything it had to offer. By nightfall, their entire generation would all be dead.

I flopped down on my bed. My butt made contact with the mattress and I winced. I'd done as Hawk had suggested and soaked in the tub last night, and then again this morning. But I was still tender between my thighs.

It wasn't painful. I felt like I'd been used. And I had been. In the span of a few hours, I'd lived more in a car garage surrounded by sexy, street racer mechanics than I had in my whole life.

Every time that I sat on a wooden bench or on a plastic chair and felt the twinge of their use, I could only smile. While my classmates rushed around harried, trying to gather data about the swarming mayflies, I'd been caught up in memories of being swarmed by four men, of mounting over half of them, and of being sent soaring.

I hoped it wouldn't be the only day I lived my life on such a frenzied high. I couldn't wait to take flight again.

I checked my phone for the hundredth time. Hawk still hadn't called or texted. He'd said he'd pick me up to take me to his party. Maybe he'd changed his mind? Maybe he'd forgotten all about me?

Well if he had forgotten, he still had my car. I'd just go and pick it up tomorrow...and likely walk in on him fucking some other girl or adulterous wife.

I turned the television on to distract myself. The newscasters were showing footage of the mayfly swarm. I'd left the lab less than an hour ago and the mating event was already over. The decaying carcasses of the insects littered the water, the forest, and in some cases, the streets. The newscaster showed footage from an hour ago of the swarm in action.

Contrary to popular belief, mayflies weren't first born and later dead on the same day. They spent the first few months, or in some cases years, of their lives underwater or beneath decaying matter. Then, when they were of mating age, they'd sprout wings and take to the sky. They'd fly high for one day, mating in a swarming frenzy with one another.

There was no monogamy amongst their kind. Multiple males mated with a single female. Sometimes, males would wait their turn on top of the flying female while another buddy got it on behind her. There were even cases of male mayflies having two penises. And then, after all the hanky panky was done, and the eggs were laid, they'd all tumble to the ground, their sated bodies breaking apart on impact.

It didn't seem a bad way to go in my opinion. A sheltered life followed by one day of utter bliss.

My phone beeped. I fell out of the bed reaching for it. When I righted myself and grabbed it off my desk, I saw it was a text from Hawk.

Be outside in thirty minutes, it read.

I sprang up off the floor, all twinges and bits of pain gone. My limbs felt like new.

I went to my closet. There was hanger after hangar of prim blouses and knee-length skirts. I chose the shortest skirt I had, which came an inch above my knee, and a blouse with a low neck line that I typically wore a camisole underneath. I forewent the camisole. And the panties.

I hadn't worn panties at all last night because the fabric irritated my swollen pussy lips. I'd gone without all day, enjoying the feel of the moisture trickling between my legs. I'd been certain that one of my male classmates would scent the constant flow of arousal between my legs, or at least hear the slippery sound of my thighs slicking past one another. But, no. They'd all been intent on their data and the insect orgy up in the sky.

I pulled on the clothes and made it outside with ten minutes to spare. I hoped the evening air would cool me down a bit. My nerves were jittery as I thought about what would happen this visit with the Watchers. I'd already fucked Hawk and Eagle. I'd seen that Crow was eager for a ride. It was likely his turn next. And then there was Owl.

Silent Owl who'd never said a word to me, only

watched with that intensity. What would it feel like to have all that intensity trained on my pussy, my breasts, my mouth? Would he come closer this time? Maybe lean over my back, silently and patiently waiting his turn, as Crow fucked my breasts? I sucked the moisture off my lower lip at the thought.

Not only did I ache to be filled, I ached to be kissed too. Only Hawk had kissed me, and only that first night in the middle of the street as his boys changed my tire.

Eagle hadn't; not before or after he'd slurped up every bit of nectar between my legs. When he went to fuck me, he'd turned me around, putting my face into the hood of the car.

Crow had been more interested in kissing my breasts than my face.

Kissing or fucking, it didn't matter to me. I was just eager to take that flight again, whether it was with one or all of them.

I'd been turned on when it was just me and Eagle in the workroom. My heartbeat had sunk to my cunt when Crow and Owl came into the room and gave me their attention. I'd especially liked it when Hawk was in the room watching. I liked the feel of his eyes on me as much as I liked the feel of his hands, lips, and penis on me, in me.

It should've shocked me that I was so eager to fuck not just one of these men, but all of them. But why should it? I spent my days amongst female creatures of the animal kingdom that enjoyed a line up of males waiting for the chance to enter their core.

Thirty minutes later, standing outside, the night's air was stifling. There was no cool breeze. Instead there was a thick vibration of energy in the air. It crawled up my skin and sat heavy on my tongue making me gulp down a lungful of air.

I crunched over the decayed body of a mayfly as I made my way to the parking lot. That would be me in a matter of hours. Fucked so hard, soared so high that I'd crash down to the earth in a tangle of my own limbs. I bounced on my feet in anticipation.

I heard footsteps behind me. I turned to see Shakira walking up in a tight pair of jeans, a halter-top that pushed up her ample breasts, and ankle boots with spiky heels. I wished we were friends. I would've loved to have raided her closet for tonight.

Shakira narrowed her eyes at me as she came up to the curb. "You headed out on a school night, sis?"

"I was invited to a party." I figured she'd move on, but we stood there in silence for a moment.

Shakira crossed her arms over her chest and pursed her lips. "Your car in the shop?"

"Yeah."

More silence.

Then she turned to me, full of aggression. "I'm gonna ask you this once, and you tell me the truth, okay sis. Did you fuck Owl?"

I blinked.

"I know you fucked Hawk. He's got a thing for naive, little girls like you. Hawk likes to share. But it looks like you know that. So I'm asking, did you get passed around to Owl?"

My initial thought was to tell her it was none of her business. My second thought was to brag that yes I fucked Hawk. And yes, he passed me around to his friends. And no, I was not ashamed. But looking at Shakira under the glare of the street lamp, I saw something unexpected.

Gone was the tough-as-nails woman. There was a vulnerability to her. So instead of shutting her down, instead of bragging, I told her the truth.

"No. I didn't fuck Owl."

She sighed, but then immediately her face transformed into a smirk. As though she realized how stupid she'd been to imagine that Owl would be interested in a naive, little girl like me. It irritated me, like the underwear I'd discarded this morning.

"He was there," I said. "He watched."

Shakira stiffened. I almost told her the rest; that he'd twisted the pussy juices out of the crotch of my panties. But something in her stoic expression stopped me from going that far.

"I don't know you, Ellie. But you look like you don't have much experience with the world. So I'll do you a favor and tell you this much. A woman shouldn't have to share her man. If she shares him with another, then he never was hers to begin with."

The sound of an engine growling halted any further conversation. It wasn't Hawk's Charger that pulled up. Owl hopped out of the driver's side of a red, Honda Civic with a black dragon along each side. He didn't glance once at me. He went straight up to Shakira.

"Hey baby," he said. His voice was like silk slicing through vanilla ice cream.

Shakira jerked away from him. She crossed her arms over her chest and turned her head away. I saw a tick in her jaw.

Owl frowned. He looked my way. His eyes looked me up and down, understanding dawning on his handsome face.

He smiled at me. "Hey, Ellie. Hawk said you needed a ride."

I nodded, too hypnotized by his voice to pollute the air with my words.

He opened the rear passenger door of his car. I climbed in.

"Buckle up," he said. "It's going to be a bumpy ride."

He shut the door and went back over to Shakira. I couldn't hear their conversation. I saw Shakira get in his personal space, putting her fingers in his face. Owl remained calm, an amused smile on his lips throughout the whole ordeal. Just like the amused smile he had on his face when he'd licked the honey from my panties.

After long moments of an unintelligible, one-sided rant, Shakira finally lost steam. Owl stepped into the danger zone that was her personal space. He planted a kiss on her collarbone. Her pouting lips trembled. But when he looked at her, she pursed them together again and stood stoic. She allowed herself to be led to the front passenger door. On her way inside, she gave me the evil eye before she turned into her seat.

The drive across town was filled with the tense silence of blaring techno music. Owl put his hand on Shakira's thigh. She slapped it away. A few seconds later, he tried again. It took four tries before she let his long fingers settle in her lap. But when he tried to move his fingers into the crotch of her jeans, she pushed his hand away again and crossed her legs away from him.

I realized whatever happened tonight, I wasn't having Owl.

FOURTEEN

We drove around the garage and pulled up to the split-level house behind it. Cars were parked all along the residential street. Owl parked the car in a spot in the two-car garage. He killed the engine and then came around and opened Shakira's door. He gave her a little peck on the cheek. She didn't slap him away.

Then he came to the rear passenger door. He gave me his hand as he helped me out. He also gave me a wink before he turned his attention back to Shakira.

I followed the two into the house. The music bounced off the walls, vibrating all around me. The air was even thicker inside the house than it was outside. The atmosphere teemed with an energy that made my head feel light and my pulse quicken.

My flat shoe crunched down onto something. I looked down at the hardwood floor to see what I'd come across. It was a discarded bra. I'd stepped onto the metal clasp.

The bra was not alone. I saw a few more in various colors, shapes and sizes. There were panties too. And skirts, and shorts, and shoes.

Discarded clothing lay all over the hallway floor as though a swarm of girls had crashed into the house and all that remained of them were their pieces of clothing. I looked up to see Shakira eyeing the mass of clothing too. We looked at each other and both gulped.

We were standing in what looked to be a small nook that led to a larger living room. Owl waited patiently at the door to the inside. He looked us both in the eye. It was the same look Hawk had given me that first night. A probing look that allowed me to make a run for it if I chose. The same challenging look Eagle had given me the other day before he bent down and ate me out on the hood of my car.

I stepped up to the door without a second's hesitation.

I heard Shakira's tiny intake of breath, but then

she stepped up too. I assumed because she didn't want to be shown up by a naive, little girl.

Owl opened the door. It should not have shocked me, what I found inside. But I was the naive girl Shakira had accused me of being.

When Hawk had said he was inviting me to a party, I thought there would be hors d'ourves, light music, and causual conversation. Maybe after the party he'd take me to his room and fuck me. Probably let his boys fuck me after he'd taken his fill.

I would've been okay with that. The fact that I would've been okay with that had proven to me that I wasn't naive. But I should've known my idea of a party and these boys' idea of a party were in two different worlds. I would've never fathomed in a million years the party scene before me.

Fucking.

There were about a dozen people fucking inside the living room.

Men fucking girls.

Girls fucking men.

Girls fucking girls.

Sitting on a couch, like a king watching his subjects, was Hawk.

I watched Hawk survey the orgy of limbs before him. There were males I didn't recognize pumping into and out of the glistening, pink pussies of girls. Two girls were attached to each other at their cores, their limbs scissoring up and down and back and forth. All the pussies, I noted, were hairless. Apparently, they all got Hawk's memo. My gaze focused on the sawing action of two, thick cocks seesawing in and out of the body of one woman. Her eyes closed, her mouth open, and her torso shook from their tag team.

My eyes went back to Hawk. His sharp gaze and focus were what I imagined mine resembled when I was at work in the lab. All Hawk needed was a white lab coat to cover his bare chest and a notepad. His eyes blazed as he surveyed his kingdom, but then he looked down and the passion fell from his gaze.

There was a girl in his lap. Her head bobbing up and down. His hand rested on her head. But there wasn't a look of ecstasy on his face like when he'd been inside me yesterday. He looked… bored.

Then, as though he sensed me watching him, he looked up and caught my eyes. After a moment in which I watched the haze of boredom clear, a wolfish grin broke out over his face. He lifted the girl's head off his thick cock. Her lips glistened in confusion. He patted her head and shooed her away. Then he crooked his finger at me.

My feet were moving before I made the conscious decision to go to him. I came to stand before him. For a few seconds, we just stared at each other.

The sounds of pleasure assailed my ears. Men grunted, women squealed and moaned. There was the crack of air from someone having their ass slapped repeatedly. I tuned it all out as Hawk smiled up at me. I tried to breathe normally as I looked at him.

He tucked his dick back in his pants and then indicated the seat beside him.

I sat down.

"Hey, Ellie," he said.

"Hello, Hawk." He reached out and caught one of my stray locks of hair. "Is that your real name?"

"No." He wound my hair around his finger. "How are you feeling this evening?"

"Fine."

"You sore?"

I shook my head no, even though I felt the tenderness where he'd pounded into me the night before while I sat on the soft cushion beside him. It felt like my pussy was starving. The ache was hunger pangs and the only thing that would satisfy my appetite was this man burying the cock he'd just put away deep inside me.

Hawk's eyes scanned mine as though he were reading my every thought. He raised an eyebrow at me in challenge.

"I'm not sore," I said. "You wanna check for yourself?" I uncrossed my legs, shocked at my own audaciousness.

His face lit up like a Christmas tree at my sass. "Yeah, I think I will."

He reached his hand out. The moment it made contact with my bare knee, I jerked. He skittered his fingers up my thigh, and I trembled. His hand disappeared up my skirt and I gasped.

I looked up into his hazel eyes. There it was again, that connection I felt to this man. That link that had me spreading my virgin legs for him out in the middle of the street. That thread that left my legs spread wide after he challenged me to take Eagle's girth after my deflowering.

But then my gaze slipped past Hawk and landed on the crowd of people watching. I didn't see the familiar faces of Eagle, Crow, or Owl.

"You don't want to go somewhere else?" I asked. "Like, maybe, your bedroom?"

"Why? Are you sleepy, Ellie?"

"No, I just thought…"

"Beds are for sleeping. I want to fuck you. Would you like me to fuck you, Ellie?"

"I would. I do want you to fuck me. It's just… I don't know any of these people."

"You let me fuck you out in the middle of the street," Hawk said. "You let me fuck you in the garage in front of my boys."

"Yeah, and I liked it. I don't mind if they see me. I don't mind if they touch me. It's just these people…"

"These are my friends." Hawk's thumb crept higher up my thigh. "None of them will touch you. None of them will even approach you without my permission."

"Really? Why?"

Hawk studied me. His fingers massaged the fleshy part of my thigh. "Do you want one of them to fuck you, Ellie?"

His gaze was intense. I knew this was another test. I just wished I knew the right answer.

I went with the truth. "I want you to fuck me. I'd like Eagle to lick my cunt again."

Hawk smiled at that, his hazel eyes as bright as a street lamp at midnight.

"And Crow didn't get a turn," I continued. "I thought he might like to… tonight."

"Crow can fuck you tonight. After me." He gave me that prideful look from the other day when he insisted that I could take Eagle after he'd had me. That look he'd had after he'd turned out to be right about my being able to take both of them back to back.

"I was looking forward to Owl, but I don't think that would be a good idea with Shakira here."

Hawk laughed. "Yeah, Owl's trying his hand at monogamy. To each his own, I guess."

"But… I don't know these other people. So, if it's all right, I'd rather not fuck anyone else but you guys."

Hawk ran his other hand, the hand that wasn't up my skirt caressing my thigh, down my face. "I told you, none of them will touch you. You're Watchers' tail."

"Watchers' tail?"

"Only Watchers Crew are allowed to fuck you."

I blinked. I'd never had staunch feminist ideals. My mother was a housewife who relied solely on my father. She'd gone to a finishing school where there were classes on household management. But she expected me to go to college. Though I think she expected my major to be in finding a husband, not the study of insects. I wanted both; a career and a husband. I wanted a modern relationship, with my own source of income, bank account, and agency. Yet, the idea of being owned by these four guys; the idea of my body belonging to this man in particular, made my sore pussy throb with eagerness.

Hawk put his hands further up my skirt until he hit the sweet spot. "You're not wearing any panties, Ellie."

"The fabric was irritating me."

He tsked. "Eagle will be pissed. He's already started a collection of your panties."

I looked up and spotted Eagle on the far side of the room. He was ramming into a girl from behind. His eyes were on me though. "I don't want him to be mad at me."

"He'll be fine. Just blow him later. And don't come empty handed again."

The edict to blow Eagle didn't rattle me. It was a single word that did: *again*.

He wanted me to come back again after tonight. I was elated. I leaned in to kiss him. I'd been dreaming about having those plump lips on mine again. But Hawk reared back out of my reach, like he'd done with Mrs. Pettigrew as she left the other day.

I looked away, my cheeks burning in mortification at the rejection.

Hawk put his thumb on my chin to turn my head back around. He ran the digit over my lips, watching it go back and forth. He stared at my lips for a second, but then shook himself. He let his hand fall away and then he leaned back, away from me.

"Take off your skirt, Ellie."

FIFTEEN

"Take off your skirt, Ellie."

I looked around me. There were a lot of eyes on me. Eyes I didn't know stared at me. Some with sexual hunger, some with barely any interest, others with jealousy. Most of the jealousy was in the eyes of the other women. Even the women who were bent over getting their brains fucked out had an eye on me. It was clear they all wanted to be where I was. Sitting beside Hawk while he told me to take off my skirt.

All the girls in the room were nude or near naked. I was the most clothed person in the room. I stood on shaky legs and reached for the zipper of my skirt. Hawk sat back and watched me, watched the zipper track its way down my hip.

I spotted Crow on the other side of the room, fondling one girl's breast while another girl lay between that girl's pussy eating her out. Crow's eyes weren't on either of those girls. They were on me. My fingers went into the loose band of my skirt and I tugged downward.

On the far side of the room I caught Eagle's gaze on me. A very satisfied woman lay in a puddle of pleasure at his feet. He was wiping his huge dick off with a wet wipe, his eyes trained on my fingers.

I let my skirt drop to the floor. Eagle frowned at the sight of my bare ass. His gaze rose to mine and those dark eyes narrowed on me in displeasure. One brow rose up as though to say, "Did you just cross me?"

I heard Hawk's rumbling laughter in front of me. "Come here, sweet meat. Let me have a taste before E takes it out on your ass."

I turned from Eagle with my eyes cast down. I stepped out of my skirt, watching it pool to the ground like a discarded limb. Funny, I hadn't even taken flight yet. I stepped over my skirt, my ass and cunt bare as I headed for Hawk.

When I got to him I assumed he wanted me to sit on his lap. His legs were opened wide in a crude fashion as he leaned back, observing me. I saw his erection bulging inside his cargo pants. His zipper was still undone. I lifted my leg to climb aboard, but he caught me by the waist and turned me outward so I faced everyone in the room.

"Fuck, I love a heart-shaped ass."

Hawk raised my shirt and fingered the creases of my ass where my butt muscle and thigh met. He traced the crease from my sacrum down to my anus. He parted my cheeks bringing his face to rest on the flesh there. I knew he'd opened his mouth when I felt his warm breath behind me. He reached his tongue out and gave my anus a quick lick. My knees gave out.

Hawk straightened up and pulled me into his lap, ass first. My knees went between his open thighs. He reached down, taking a knee in each hand. He parted my legs, draping them over his spread thighs. I stiffened.

"Are you sore, sweet meat?"

"No." My voice was so small, I wasn't sure he'd heard me. I saw all eyes on me. Mostly the jealous eyes outlined in eyeliner. One girl smirked at my hesitance.

"You said you wanted me to fuck you, sweet meat." One of his hands rested on my knee, not probing any further. The other snuck under my shirt and found my nipple. "You gotta let me in if you want to get fucked."

My legs relaxed on an unconscious decision and my upper body collapsed into his. My brain focused on the fingers on my nipple, his voice at my ear, the thing he was doing with his tongue at the back of my neck. I closed my eyes. I shut out all those girls and their evil eyes and just focused on Hawk.

The fingers of his lower hand, the hand that had been resting on my knee, found their way to my swollen pussy lips. "Is it too tender, baby? You want me to stop?"

"Please don't stop, Hawk." I arched my ass back into his erection.

"You want it?" His index finger circled my clit.

I shoved my hips forward into his teasing hand. "I need it, please. I need you inside me. Please, Hawk."

I felt movement behind me. I felt his erection spring free of his pants. I felt the coolness of foil and then latex. He leaned me forward, and then he was inside me. With his thighs, he spread my knees even wider, wider for all to see. With his hand he spread the lips of my cunt so everyone saw me swelling and dripping and quivering as he pumped into me.

"You tell them who this belongs to, Ellie." Hawk

covered my pussy with his big palm. Then he used his fingers to pull the lips of my core apart.

"It's yours," I panted.

"No."

"It's Watchers'. I'm Watchers' tail."

"Good girl."

It felt like everyone in the room had stopped what they were doing to watch us. I didn't like it as much as the day before. There was judgment and envy in their eyes. There had been nothing but appreciation, eagerness, when the guys looked at me.

Then Eagle came into my view, followed by Crow. I focused on them as Hawk pummeled into me. Looking at their hungry gazes sent me over the cliff. Hawk roared as I clenched around him. He buried his face between my shoulder blades as he jerked once, twice, a third time into me, spilling his seed. He held me close to him, his teeth pressed into my spine as we caught our breath.

When I came back to consciousness, Crow smiled and held out his arms. "My turn."

Crow lifted me off Hawk. I looked back to see Hawk looking after me. His expression looked like the intersection between satisfaction, desire, and devastation.

Crow laid me down on the wooden coffee table

in front of Hawk. He unbuttoned my shirt and spread it wide. He dispensed of my bra one-handed and my breasts spilled out to the sides. Crow was already naked. His thick penis head was nearly red with tension.

He came over top of me and bent down. "Hey, Ellie," he grinned.

I couldn't help myself, I grinned back. "Hey, Crow."

"I'm gonna fuck your titties now, okay?"

"Okay."

He winked at me with that boyish grin. He put his pink dick between my breasts. "Push them together for me, Ellie."

I did as he asked and squeezed my breasts around his penis. Crow closed his eyes in ecstasy. He pumped between my breasts. It wasn't very arousing, the thrusting between my breasts. But the joy on his face was wonderful to watch. His penis head poked at my chin with each stroke.

"Open your mouth, sweet meat. Have a taste."

That came from Hawk who lounged back in his chair watching the two of us. I did as Hawk said. Every time Crow thrust, I got a taste of his pink penis head. It was salty and sweet at the same time. I'd expected to be disgusted by the taste of a man's semen, but I wasn't. I liked it. I anticipated it, reach for it every time Crow thrust. I tried to catch him with my lips instead of just my tongue.

Crow reached back and put his fingers inside my cunt. He got one, two, three thick fingers inside me. Then he curled his fingers in that come-hither motion that Eagle had used to set the floodgates rushing inside me the other day. Crow knocked on that same door.

On its own, my head lifted off the table to chase his penis. My hips tilted up to meet his hand. Before I could process it happening, my hips shook with an orgasm. I hadn't even noticed it building. It came out of nowhere. I let go of my breasts and grabbed Crow's penis, sucking the head deep into my throat as I rode out the waves of pleasure.

Crow reared back with a roar. He took his penis out of my hands and aimed it at my breasts. He sprayed his semen across my breasts with a long stream. When he finished, his body was bent over mine as though broken.

I reached up to touch his face out of concern. He grinned into my palm, giving it a wet kiss.

Hawk handed Crow a wet wipe, and he cleaned my breasts. Crow's happy face was a little sad as he cleaned his semen from my breasts. When I was all tidied up, he bent down and kissed each of my nipples in turn. Then he looked up at me with a smile. He leaned into my face. I rose to give him a kiss, but Crow was shoved back before he could reach my lips.

Hawk glared at him. His hand thrust up between Crow and I like a stop-in-the-name-of-love motion. Crow smirked, but he backed off.

A dark cloud moved into his space. Eagle stood over me, his arms crossed over his chest, his face stern. I felt at any moment, he'd swoop down and carry me off like a piece of meat.

SIXTEEN

Eagle tore his gaze from me and looked to Hawk. Hawk sat back in his chair, his legs still spread in the lewd fashion as when he'd fucked me. Another silent conversation passed between Hawk and Eagle. Finally, Hawk made a motion for Eagle to proceed.

Eagle bent down, his large form obstructed my view of everyone and everything in the room. Without any effort, he raised my body up and into a sitting position.

Eagle crouched down before me, eyes on me, unflinching. "Where are your panties, sweet meat?"

There was a warning note to his tone. The instinct in prey to flee at the sound of danger rang loud in my ears.

"I…" I looked to Hawk who only offered me a

raised eyebrow and a smirk. "They were irritating me. So, I took them off. I'm sorry."

Eagle frowned. The look he gave me reminded me of the looks teachers gave wayward students who'd forgotten their homework, and then came up with lame excuses.

"I won't forget next time, Eagle. Would you like me to lick your penis in penance?"

Eagle quirked a brow. "Penance? You mean for a punishment? Sucking my dick is a reward, sweet meat."

"Is there anything I can do to make it up to you? To earn that reward."

Eagle smiled. It was a cruel smile. It sent my heartbeat down to my cunt. Whatever punishment he'd thought up for me, I knew I wanted it. Knew I would like it.

"Be cool, E," Hawk said. "She's still a little bit of a virgin."

"There's no such thing as a little bit of a virgin. She's broken in." Eagle turned back to me. "I'm not the one to baby you, sweet meat. You need to learn that when you come to someone's party, you bring the host a gift."

He spread my thighs. There was a puddle of my excitement on the wood table.

"You came to my house empty handed. I won't tolerate bad manners, sweet meat." Eagle stared me in the eye. It was the same look as yesterday. He was waiting to see if I'd bolt.

"Is there anything I can offer you... to make up for it?"

If the devil had a smile, he'd learned it from Eagle. "Go lean over the couch."

I rose and did as he told me. I was completely nude in a room full of people who were either watching me get fucked, or they were getting fucked themselves. I heard girls climaxing, boys grunting. I heard the slaps of spanking. The rhythmic scrapings of furniture legs scooting across the floor from thrusting power. Then I heard a buzzing behind me.

It brought my mind to the beehive. Just like in the hive, there were more females here than there were males. Unlike in the hive, more than one female was getting serviced by the males. The queen bee didn't share. But research also proved that the queen didn't take over a hive by force. No, she did it by stealth. Sneaking in at night to a colony without a queen, catching the men off guard, and then establishing herself as their ruler. Drones were like moths to flames in the presence of a queen. Crow and Hawk sat back with their eyes riveted on my body.

I jumped when the buzzing made contact with my leg. It wasn't a bee that landed on my thigh. It was a small vibrator. It was metallic, silver, and shaped like an egg. A cord came from it. Attached to the other end of the cord was a rectangular remote control.

I'd never used a vibrator. I hadn't known what a dildo was until my freshman year in college when I accidentally stumbled across my roommate's Rabbit which she'd left in the shower. I'd never even masturbated, not because my parents had taught me it was a sin. They'd never taught me anything about sex at all. I'd never taken matters into my own hands because, quite frankly, I hadn't known what to do.

Eagle ran the egg up my thigh. He pressed it to my clit. I cried out and buckled over the couch.

He tsked me, shaking his head. "I thought you were serious about making things up to me, Ellie. I told you to lean over the couch, not lay down on it."

He said this all while keeping the vibrating egg pressed against my clit. I'd barely understood the words coming out of his mouth. It was with great difficulty that I straightened my body to come back up to a kneeling position.

Eagle removed the vibrator from my clit. My

moment of relief was short lived. He parted my pussy lips and worked the small vibrator inside me.

My eyes opened wide. I looked over to Hawk. He leaned back in the chair, watching Eagle's handiwork as though he were watching his new favorite television show and didn't want to be disturbed. I saw he would be no help.

Crow stood off to the side of me. His blurry movements told me he was bouncing on his toes at the show.

Eagle slipped a new pair of panties over my legs. They were simple cotton panties. White, utilitarian, no lace or g-string. He pulled the top of the waste band up, making sure that the cotton would hold the egg rooted firmly inside of me with no chance of slipping out. My world tuned to the buzzing inside of me.

"Your penance, sweet meat, is to come in these panties. Drip that sweet juice all over the crotch. After your third go, I'll let you-"

I moaned deep as an orgasm wracked through my body.

Hawk burst out laughing.

Crow applauded and hooted.

Eagle sighed. "After two more goes, I'll let you suck my dick."

It was a strain to open my eyes as I was still throbbing from that last orgasm. The buzzing inside of me that had caused it did not cease. When I finally managed to have a look at my surroundings, the first thing I saw was that Eagle held the rectangular remote control in his hand. The dials went from 1 to 4. It was currently on 1. He turned it up to 2.

The buzzing increased. My eyes widened, and I gripped the back of the couch. I looked to Hawk. He leaned his head in his hand, gazing at me as though I were the best entertainment he'd seen in a long time. A girl approached him, offering him her bare cunt. He ignored her, his eyes trained on me.

Hawk nodded his head at me, rhythmically, as though he were chanting or cheering me on. I stared at his lips. He appeared to be mouthing the words "Come on." I rocked my hips to and fro in time with his soundless chant. Before I knew it my hips were gyrating to their own rhythm as another orgasm seized my body.

Hawk sighed along with me. His large body collapsed back into the seat as my body slumped over the couch.

"Fuck, look at her nipples," said Crow. "They

look like pink rocks. Yo E, let me get another taste man?"

"Knock yourself out, bruh."

I looked up to Eagle, my eyes and mouth trembling along with the aftershocks of two orgasms so close together. "I can't... I can't do another."

Eagle cocked his head to the side. It was the same motion I'd seen a bird of prey perform as he tuned his senses in the search for his next meal. "Did you not just offer me penance? Did you not just ask me what you could do to make it better?"

My brain was too fogged to unravel the double negatives.

"You're the one who came into my house empty handed, sweet meat."

"I didn't know..." I panted.

"And now you do," Eagle turned the dial up to three.

I screamed. My fingers gripped the cushion. I clamped my thighs together trying to dull the sensations inside me. It didn't help. I looked up in a desperate plea, but all I got in return was a wicked grin. Now I knew what was on the other side of the wariness buried in the lines of Eagle's face.

Hawk chuckled. "E, you fucking, sadistic bastard."

Crow sat down on the couch. He pulled me up and draped my body over his. Just the touch of his hand on my thighs was too much. Before he even put his mouth anywhere near my breasts, a third orgasm ripped through my body.

I was trembling, shaking, delirious. When I caught my breath and a semblance of sense, Crow looked crestfallen. He looked to Eagle like a petulant child.

Eagle shrugged. "Make it four."

Crow grinned like Eagle had just given him a piece of candy. Tears streamed down my eyes as Crow's tongue reached for my breasts.

"I can't," I pleaded. "Oh god, I can't."

Crow ignored my pleas. It wasn't hard to see why. The moment he made contact with my breasts, my fingers dug into his scalp clutching him to me as he sucked, flicked, and laved.

My hips developed a mind of their own as they jerked a dance in his lap. I needed to press them together to find relief, but Crow kept them forced apart with his legs. I looked to Eagle whose thumb hovered on the dial as though he were debating whether or not to turn it up the final notch. I looked over to Hawk who squirmed on his throne, his knuckles caught in his teeth, his erection protruding from his pants.

I focused on Hawk. On the connection I felt with him.

"Come on, sweet meat," Hawk whispered. Or maybe I imagined him saying it.

In any case, I did what he asked.

I came.

Hard.

SEVENTEEN

The ringing in my ears stopped. The buzzing at my core stopped.

"Dude, she fucking creamed all over me." Crow put my head in the crook between his neck and shoulder and stroked my hair. "You did good, Ellie."

I relaxed in Crow's warm embrace until my chest stopped heaving and I began to breathe normally. As soon as my breathing settled, I felt something warm and wet poke my lips.

"Here's your reward, sweet meat."

I looked up at Eagle. His thick, dick was monstrous before my eyes. The pink head topping the dark brown was a thing of beauty. I took a moment to marvel at it before I opened my mouth.

He slid his penis inside, just past the tip. It was warm and salty on my tongue.

Eagle pulled out before I was ready. I closed my lips around him and he came out of my mouth with a pop.

"Open," he said.

I did as I was told.

"Give me your tongue. Tilt your head back."

Once I'd followed his instructions, Eagle ran his cock back and forth over my tongue.

"Keep your mouth open. Relax."

I did as he said. He went in and out, slowly. With each steady thrust he went a little further. The rhythmic motions were lulling.

When Hawk had shoved his dick down Mrs. Pettigrew's throat it looked arduous, painful. This was easy. This was nice. I relaxed into the support of Crow's neck while he stroked my hair and Eagle pumped in and out of me. I flicked my tongue to get more of Eagle's salty musk and he groaned.

I opened my eyes wide, wondering if I would get reprimanded. Eagle had said to keep my mouth open. But no reprimand came. Eagle's eyes were heavy, hazy. I took advantage.

I hollowed my cheeks and sucked. There was not much give with his massive size. My tongue traced the thick veins on the underside of his cock when he thrust deep. I laved at the soft flesh of his cockhead when he withdrew. My tongue caught in the divot before he thrust back in.

Eagle grabbed the back of the couch and pumped faster. I felt him swelling on my tongue. At the first drop of his semen, I startled. I'd been so caught up in the feel of his flesh I'd forgotten all about the end game.

Eagle roared as his seed pumped out of him and onto my tongue. He coated my tongue and filled my jaws. He spent himself completely inside of my mouth before he withdrew. I felt all their eyes on me waiting to see what I'd do with a mouthful of his semen.

I closed my mouth and swallowed, reveling in the creamy texture as it traveled down my throat. I gulped and took in a breath of air. When I was done, it felt like the guys let out a collective sigh of release.

"HEY, I'm about to take Kira home. You want me to take her too?"

My eyes were closed, but I recognized the silky soft timbre of Owl's voice.

"No, I got her. She can sleep it off and drive herself home in the morning." That was Hawk's gruff voice.

My eyes struggled open as I stretched my limbs. I must've passed out on the couch after sucking off Eagle. But I wasn't on the couch anymore. I was airborne.

My chest was leaned up against a pillow, a warm pillow with hard angles. From the corner of my eye, I recognized Hawk's pecs. I was in his arms. He was carrying me out of the living room. All the bodies and clothes were gone. The room was empty. It resembled a normal, every day living room from an urban catalog.

We were in a hallway, headed for a staircase. I caught sight of Shakira and Owl leaving through the front door. Shakira looked at me in Hawk's arms. She pursed her lips together, but said nothing. I wonder where she and Owl had disappeared off to during the party. I hadn't seen either of them once.

It didn't matter. I was sure I disagreed with her about sharing men and being shared. She didn't know what she was missing. She'd thought I was a naive, little girl. But it looked like I was staying for longer than lunch, longer than dinner even. I was

Watchers' tail. I'd be around in the morning for breakfast.

Hawk brought me up the stairs to what I had to assume was his bedroom. The lights were off, but I could make out dark furniture. A huge sleigh bed, a chest of drawers. There were no curtains on the windows and the blinds were open to the moon's light and any neighbors' gazes.

Hawk laid me down on the massive bed. Then he disappeared inside what had to be a connecting bathroom. I heard the faucet running. He reemerged with a wet hand towel. He ran the towel all over my body, cleaning up the remnants of the party off me. My body was too sore and numb to take any pleasure from it.

When he was done he tossed the cloth back into the bathroom. Then he turned and peered down at me. "You ready to go to bed, Ellie?"

"With you? I thought you didn't do sleepovers."

He shrugged. "I don't fuck in my bed. I sleep in my bed. You're in no condition to drive yourself home and I'm tired. I don't feel like driving you home."

I didn't mention that Owl had just offered me a ride and Hawk had refused it. "You're right," I said instead. "I don't think I could make it home tonight."

He slipped under the covers behind me. "Good night, sweet meat."

"Good night, Hawk."

He gathered the covers around us and pulled me back into his hips into a spoon. I heard his rhythmic breathing a moment later letting me know he'd fallen asleep. Then I was out too.

I dreamed about them. All four of them taking me in turns, Owl included, with Shakira watching while standing outside looking in through a window. Hawk fucked into my cunt. Eagle's head was in my lap licking my clit. Crow had his dick between my breasts. Owl? Owl whispered naughty things in my ear with that silky voice of his. It all felt so real. I felt the wetness between my thighs. I felt the pressure of something massive entering me.

My eyes opened. A large mass was over top of me, parting my thighs. Hawk put his massive cock inside me. I was sore, but I was no longer numb. I opened for him without protest. We both groaned when he was fully seated inside me. We stayed that way for long moments. I felt his heart beating through the pulsing of his thick penis inside my tight pussy. I felt his actual heart beating as his chest rested above mine.

His eyes had been closed, but now they were

open. He stared down at me as though he was waking from a dream too, and he was surprised to see me there in the flesh.

His dick throbbed inside of me. He brought his hand up to my face. He reached out his thumb and traced my lower lip. More than anything I wanted to reach down and suck it into my mouth. But I didn't. I held still and waited for him. And then it happened.

He leaned in, so slowly I was afraid to move lest I scare him away. The impact of his lips against mine brought out a sob from my chest. He ran his lips over mine, tentatively, as though testing for their realness. Then he moved his hips and his tongue in tandem. Both in a slow, swirling motion that sent me into orbit. It was heaven on earth. I wrapped my legs around his torso, my arms around his neck. I gave over to him completely.

"*Dios mio,*" he whispered. "What the fuck are you doing to me?"

We rode together into oblivion under the cover of night. After we both came on silent cries that rang deep into the depths of us, we both fell back into a deep sleep. Mine was dreamless this time.

When the sun woke me in the morning, my first thought was that I'd dreamed what had happened between us in his bed. Hawk had told me flat out he didn't do romance or sleepovers or sex in a bed.

When I rolled over, he was there, awake, alert, and staring at me. Before I could get out a good morning, Hawk's face was above mine and his body was between my thighs. His tongue and his dick slid deep inside me.

EIGHTEEN

I felt the sun creep in through the windows. The rays touched my face, kissing my forehead, my eyelashes, my cheeks. The brightness level rose higher, going lower down my body and warming my breasts, my belly, my legs. Somehow the rays snuck in between my legs and spread its delicious, wet warmth there. It flicked its rays over my clit and-

My eyes opened wide as my legs were parted. I saw a jean clad ass in the air, crawling up under the covers.

"Morning, sweet meat," Eagle said from beneath the covers in between a mouthful of my warm cunt.

"Awww," was my reply.

My head fell back on the pillow, but it didn't land on something soft. I turned my head to see

Hawk dozing peacefully beside me. On Eagle's next tongue flick, I gasped.

Hawk's eyes slowly opened and focused on me. He tilted his head down to the body beneath the sheets. Then quirked an eyebrow at me. I grasped his forearm as Eagle swirled his tongue around my clit.

Hawk rose on his elbow and watched my body undulate to Eagle's ministrations. He reached over and ran his thick forefinger over the parted lips of my mouth.

The sheet covered Eagle's upper body. I couldn't see what he was doing or anticipate his moves. He had my ass in a vice grip and complete control of my hips and pussy. I moaned deep as he covered my entire vagina with his mouth and slurped.

Hawk chuckled. "Fuck, I love that sound. You like that sound, sweet meat?"

My answer was unintelligible. Hawk ran his fingers lightly over my face, tracing the outline of my open mouth. Eagle sucked on my clitoris, exaggerating the audio effects. I whimpered helplessly, pleading with my eyes as I looked at Hawk.

Hawk's fingers continued their journey over the planes of my face. He was now at my eyelids, running his forefinger lightly over my lashes. He traced the crinkles at the edges. His own eyes narrowed in wonder, locked on my every motion and cry. His tongue swayed back and forth over the tip of his upper lip. His tongue's movements were in tune with my whimpers as though he was the conductor and my mouth was the instrument. He seemed hypnotized.

Eagle stuck his tongue deep into my core, his nose rubbed at my clit.

I gasped, but I didn't break eye contact with Hawk. Hawk inhaled the breath that escaped my gasping mouth as though he could taste the sensations swirling inside me. I was close. I knew they both sensed it.

Hawk's jaw tensed. He snuck a glance down at the sheet-clad body between my legs. Then turned back to me. Like a thief in the night, he stole down to my mouth and nibbled at the corner of my lips as I panted.

But he did not kiss me. Not like last night. The tease of his lips was more than I could handle. Every time I tried to turn my face into his to catch his lips, he withdrew and went to the opposite side of my face. I didn't understand why he wouldn't kiss me again. My brain couldn't offer any cells to ponder it.

When Eagle pushed me over the cliff, Hawk

captured my lips and devoured my cries of ecstasy. His tongue fell in tune with Eagle's machinations, only Hawk sought deeper into me, his tongue trying to touch my soul. I reached up and pulled his head down to mine trying to give him what we needed. He let me, threading his hand through my hair and clenching me to him.

A throat cleared above us.

Hawk jerked away from my lips as though they were fire. We broke apart to find Eagle wiping his mouth.

"If you two are finished braiding each other's hair..." Eagle drawled.

Hawk sobered. "What the fuck do you want, E?"

Eagle tsked with a grin on his face. "Somebody woke up on the wrong side of the bed."

Hawk growled, aggression rolling off of him where there had been tenderness before.

Eagle smirked. He lowered himself down on top of me. His lower body pressed my knees open wider. The heft of him felt good between my legs. He hovered over my lips without touching them.

Hawk growled beside him.

Eagle only grinned. He brushed a stray hair from my lips with his fingertips. He turned to Hawk while he toyed with my nipples. "You got a visitor."

"I'm unavailable right now," Hawk snarled.

"You sure? It's scheduled maintenance."

Hawk spared me a glance before he rolled off the bed. His face was closed off.

"You sleep well, sweet meat?" Eagle asked.

I turned my attention back to Eagle who traced the outline of my breast. "I did. Thank you for the wake up call."

Eagle grinned. I noticed he had dimples on both sides of his cheeks. It made him even more devastating. "That's what I like about you, sweet meat. You got manners. You show your appreciation."

"Unlike some assholes who barge in without knocking." Hawk pulled a t-shirt over his massive frame.

"Never needed to knock before," said Eagle. "You never had anyone spend the night before. I don't think you've ever fucked in this room? Unless it was your right hand."

Hawk's jaw tensed the more Eagle talked. I heard his teeth grinding. "Ellie, get dressed. Eagle will get your car ready."

I made to sit up and winced.

"Poor girl's pussy has been used good," said Eagle. "Did you give her a soak?"

Hawk's looked away, shame-faced.

Eagle tsked again. "See what I mean, Ellie? No manners."

Hawk made to step towards Eagle.

Eagle rose from the bed to meet him.

"I'll run her a bath." The silky voice came from the doorway. Owl stood in the hall, bare chested. Hair sleep mussed.

Hawk didn't spare me another glance. He stormed out the room with a grinning Eagle in his wake.

Owl regarded me from the doorway, looking me up and down. It was then I remembered I was completely naked in Hawk's bed. Owl crossed the room and headed for the bathroom.

I heard the sound of the water running. I got up, wrapping a sheet around me and went into the bathroom.

Owl sat on the toilet seat adding oils and salt to the bath. He looked up at me and quirked an eyebrow. I followed his teasing glance to my hands clutched around the sheet.

He'd seen me naked. Everyone who'd been in the house had seen me naked. I had nothing to hide. I let the sheet fall to the ground.

Owl held my hand like a gentleman and brought

me into the bathroom. He closed the door behind me.

"If you're going to be fucking this much you need to start a soaking regimen," he said.

I made a note of the brands of oils and bath salts lined up on the bathroom cabinet because I fully intended to be fucking this much.

I looked back at the closed door and hesitated. "Where's Shakira?"

"Home."

"You didn't sleep over there with her?"

"I'm not a teenaged girl, Ellie. I don't do sleepovers. Plus, I prefer to sleep alone."

Hawk had said something similar the other night, that he didn't do sleepovers. But here I was getting out of his bed this morning.

"Will she get mad?" I asked. "Shakira. Will she get mad if she finds out?"

"Finds out what?" Owl frowned. His eyes roamed leisurely and unapologetically over my flushed breasts and bare pussy. "I'm not going to fuck you, Ellie."

I felt a supreme sense of disappointment at that statement.

"I'm just giving you a bath. So, there's nothing for her to find out about."

The tub filled. He held out his hand and helped me into the basin. The water was hot, but amazing on my aching core and limbs. It smelled divine, like a bouquet of flowers. I slipped under the waves of the water and felt at home. I closed my eyes.

This was how I wanted to go to sleep every night, cradled in Hawk's arms while he fucked me slowly. I wanted to wake up every morning to Eagle slipping between my thighs and licking my cunt. I was hoping to walk down the stairs and find Crow lying in wait to pounce on my chest and suck my nipples for breakfast. And then, after the fucking festivities, I wanted Owl to run me a bath to soothe my aches and pains. All so I could get up and do it all over again.

But then I remembered. My dream wouldn't be happening this weekend. I was supposed to go away with my boyfriend, Jerry. He'd booked a cabin where we would spend the night and have sex for the first time. Both of us were supposed to lose our virginities together.

I hadn't even thought about Jerry in the past couple of days. I couldn't go away with him now, not since I'd already lost my virginity the other night. Not since I'd already fucked not one, not two, but three guys and had no plans to stop any time soon.

Wait.

My math was wrong.

It was more than three guys that had made themselves at home in between my legs. It was now four guys. I let out a sigh of pleasure as Owl's hand slip between my legs.

NINETEEN

I opened my eyes to see Owl peering between my thighs. "You look sore, Ellie. You should probably keep your legs closed for a day or two, if you know what I mean."

I frowned at his prognosis. I had no intentions of closing my legs to Hawk anytime soon. In fact, I was eager for him to get back from the shop so we could have some afternoon delight.

Owl looked down at me and laughed. It was clear those eyes saw more than he ever had occasion to say.

"Hawk is like any man, he likes the chase. Don't make it too easy for him." Owl's hand caressed the inside of my thigh, dangerously close to my outer labia.

I thought about those words as Owl moved his hand down to massage the skin where my thigh met my butt. "Is that why you want Shakira? Because she makes you chase after her?"

Owl smiled, but he didn't answer me. His eyes crinkled when he smiled. His fingers grazed over my swollen pussy and went to the other thigh. His strong hands worked the muscles there.

"She seems very territorial." I thought about her demands to know if I was fucking Owl. "So you two are…?" I let my sentence trail off hoping Owl would pick up the definition of his relationship with Shakira.

He chuckled, a low grumbling sound that I felt in my core as his wrist grazed the sensitive flesh there. "Exactly," he said. "We are a set of ellipses. As yet to be defined."

His voice was so soothing. He was likely to lull me back to sleep if I kept listening to him talk.

"How do you want to be defined?" I asked, mostly just to keep myself conscious. Between his roving fingers and his hypnotic voice, I was liable to sink down into the tub and drown in absolute ecstasy.

Owl shrugged. "I like Shakira. I like fucking her.

She doesn't like when I fuck other girls. I want to keep on fucking her. So..."

"So you're not fucking other girls so long as you want to keep fucking her?"

"That's right."

"And when you want to start fucking other girls?"

His thumb traced the outline of one of my labials. "If I want to start fucking other girls, I'll tell her and we'd probably stop seeing each other."

He pulled my fleshy skin between his thumb and forefinger, working it back and forth. I raised my eyebrows at him in question.

"I'm not fucking you, Ellie. Trust me, you'd be screaming for more if I were fucking you."

"Then what are you doing?"

"You're sore. I'm giving you a massage. Helping you work out the kinks. I'm sure you'd do the same for me if I pulled a muscle or had a cramp." He rubbed his thumb in a circle around the folds of my pussy. "Plus, if I were fucking you, I'd make sure you came."

Owl's fingers stretched my pussy lips. The circular, kneading motion just as hypnotic as his voice. As he made bigger circles, he grazed my swollen clit. I couldn't speak. I bit my lip.

"You're not gonna come, are you Ellie? Because if I fuck a girl, I always make her come. It would be rude not to and I was raised with manners. Only an inconsiderate, selfish prick would leave a girl high and dry between her legs."

I began moving my hips in time with his pussy massage. He moved his fingers back to my outer lips and pressed on the muscles between my thighs. He drove me insane. Every time I came close to coming, he'd change tactics, change the pressure of his fingers, change the area of his focus. By the time he was finished torturing me, the water was cool but my body was steaming hot.

Owl got up and pulled the plug. The water left the tub in a rush. I was left feeling ready to burst if a soft breeze blew my way.

Owl helped me out of the tub. My legs wouldn't support me and I collapsed into his arms. He smiled down at me. There was what looked like care and tenderness on his face. I wrapped my arms around his neck. I pressed my body into his, feeling his erection. I leaned in to his lips and-

"Whoa, Ellie. What are you doing?" He held me away from him, looking at me as though I'd lost my mind.

I was dumbfounded, aroused, frustrated and confused.

"Kissing is something guys do with their girls, not with a piece of tail. No offense."

I forced my legs to work, and I stepped back. Hawk had kissed me that first night. He hadn't kissed me in the orgy, but he did last night when we were alone. And again this morning when he thought Eagle wasn't looking. He'd gotten pissed when it looked like Crow was getting too close to my lips last night, and again this morning when Eagle hovered over my lips.

But he had kissed me. It had to mean something.

Owl leaned down and kissed my forehead. "Come on, let's get you dressed."

Owl toweled me off, spending a lot of time on my breasts and ass. He tried to make my pussy dry but with each swipe of the terry cloth, I only got wetter and wetter. He gave up with a wicked smile and led me back into the bedroom. He dressed me in my own clothes; bra, skirt, blouse. No panties. They were tithed to Eagle.

He walked me down the stairs with a hand on my lower back. That hand felt like a sensual weight that I wanted to sink lower.

We walked out of the house and across the road

to the garage. I saw my car parked on the street, ready to go.

When we got inside the garage, Crow leaned back on the bench just as he'd been when Hawk took my virginity. Eagle leaned against a wall. In the center of the room stood a scantily clad woman. Her hands were on Hawk's chest, making clear suggestions.

Hawk watched her impassively. The same bored expression he'd worn last night before he'd spotted me standing in his living room. The girl leaned into his face as though she would kiss him. Hawk jerked back with a wince of disgust. Eagle chuckled. Hawk turned and scowled at him.

But then, as though he sensed me coming in, Hawk's eyes shot up to me. My heart skipped a beat when his dark eyes landed on me. I watched him do a heated scan of my body. I felt hot everywhere his eyes touched me. When he reached my face again, I smiled up at him. Something unreadable passed over his features. It was as though his face shuttered, like he'd closed the metal doors on the garage.

He looked away from me and reached out to the girl. He grabbed her by her upper arms and spun her around. He shoved her into the wall and hefted her skirt.

My legs stopped moving.

Hawk pulled down the girl's thong. Not all the way down, just enough so that her pussy was exposed. The girl's eyes closed in ecstasy, her grin spread as wide as her legs.

Hawk hastily undid his belt and pulled out his dick. He grabbed a condom from his back pocket, strapped it on, and rammed his dick up the girl's pussy. It all happened so fast.

The girl howled in pleasure. Crow applauded in a slow gulf clap. "Yeah, make those titties bounce, Hawk."

Eagle laughed and turned his back on the scene. He winked at me as he passed by me and headed back into the office.

Hawk pumped his dick brutally into the girl. She sang a chorus of *harder, harder, harder*. He did so. His thrusts were so hard they slammed her repeatedly into the wall.

"You like that?" Hawk slapped her ass. The loud crack broke through the air. "Whose pussy is this?"

"It's yours, Hawk. It's your pussy. Only yours."

I felt light-headed. I realized it was because I was panting. Not the good kind of panting that I'd done last night and this morning. The smell of raw sex saturated the atmosphere. I couldn't get enough clean air down my lungs and I refused to take in any more of the stench.

A pair of arms came around me from behind. "Hey, sweet meat. You're still here." Crow's hands found my breasts. He pinched my nipples. But it felt wrong. It all felt wrong.

Hawk looked over at me just then as he pumped into the girl, driving her to orgasm. I broke free of Crow's hold.

"What's the matter, sweet meat?" Crow called from behind me.

"I have to get to class," I called over my shoulder as I hurried for the door.

I headed out to my car. Once outside, I took in gulps of fresh air, trying to fill my lungs and clear my head. I rubbed my eyes against the glare of the sun trying to wipe the sight of Hawk fucking another girl in front of me out of my mind.

Had he wanted me to like it?

Should I have liked it?

He'd spent the night watching his boys fuck me. It was clear to see that he'd liked watching that. I'd seen the ecstasy in his eyes as he'd watched me soar with Crow and Eagle's dicks in me. It was as though he shared my pleasure, took joy in it. It was as though he wanted his boys to push me higher than he could on his own.

I'd seen him fucking Mrs. Pettigrew the day before. I'd seen him with a girl in his lap as I came into the party. But watching him with that girl just now? It felt wrong. Something about the way he'd looked at me before he'd taken her, the way he'd looked at me as he was ramming into her, it made my stomach hurt.

I yanked at the door of my car. The door wouldn't budge. I remembered I'd given Eagle my keys when I left my car here for servicing. I closed my eyes and leaned against my car. I did not want to go back in there to the garage.

I heard a jangle behind me.

I steeled myself. I did not want to face Hawk. I couldn't even tell myself to put my big girl panties on. Eagle had them. I turned around. A brown hand held my keys out to me.

"You'd have figured it out sooner or later, sweet meat," Eagle said. "He's an asshole that'll fuck anything with a warm cunt. We're all assholes that'll fuck anything with a warm cunt."

I thought back to last night when Eagle had had his dick buried up some girl's ass. Hawk had had some girl in his lap. Crow had had two girls on him.

Owl had been pressed up against Shakira last night too, but he'd had his hands between my thighs this morning. There had been a house full of girls eager to get their chance at any of their cocks.

If they wanted to share me, it meant I had to share them too. Could I do that?

"You're not cut out for this life, sweet meat. You got mono written all over you. Mono and marriage and babies and picket fences and shit. Go home, sweet heart. Before you get hurt."

The wariness was gone from Eagle's eyes. He didn't look defensive for once. He looked sad.

I reached out and took my car keys.

"But fuck if I won't miss that sweet cunt you got between your legs."

Eagle took my chin between his thumb and forefinger. He laid the lightest kiss on my lips. Then he turned and went back into the garage. From the distance, I heard the sound of the girl climaxing.

I got in my car and went home.

TWENTY

I skipped class. It was the first time in four years. But hey, I was on a role with first time experiences this week.

My first orgasm had been out in the middle of a dark street.

My loss of virginity had been on the hood of a car.

My first blowjob had been in a room full of strangers.

On the scale of badass, playing hooky from the final few days of my senior classes was peanuts.

I rolled over on my mattress and winced. I was still a bit sore despite Owl's soothing bath and massage. Sorer than my pussy were my feelings.

I scratched at the irritation in my chest. Every

time I closed my eyes, I saw Hawk looking at me while he fucked that girl. His expression unreadable but holding me still, making sure I watched. I could no longer tell if I was hurt that he'd fucked her in front of me? Or if I was just jealous that he'd fucked her instead of me? It didn't matter. I wasn't going back to get fucked again.

The space between my legs, which had been a sore spot only a moment ago, throbbed in excitement at the thought of getting fucked again. I clamped down on my feelings and I squeezed my thighs together. My resolve strengthened as the throbbing subsided. I was nearly back to myself, back to my calm, quiet, plain, predictable self.

My phone rang. I leaped for it. The name on the caller ID was not who my heart pounded for.

It was Jerry, my boyfriend. My boyfriend who I was supposed to go away with tomorrow for a weekend of planned romance and intercourse.

What was I going to do about Jerry? I had to tell him. But tell him what? That I'd fucked a group of guys and it had been a mistake? That I'd been about to throw everything I'd worked for four years for away on a couple of orgasms?

Okay, a lot of orgasms.

I was not this girl. I had a plan. A three story

home, two children, and one devoted husband. Not a life in a crowded garage with a host of strangers fucking anything with a warm cunt. My initial plan could still work. I answered the phone.

"Hey Jer -Jerry."

"Eleanor, hey. I was just checking in. You've had truffles before, right?"

"Um...yeah?"

"Good, I picked up some for this weekend. They're supposed to be an aphrodisiac. I thought... well, you know. We could have some and then..."

Hawk had never offered me an aphrodisiac. He'd never even offered me a glass of water. No, he'd just put his hands down my panties and I got aroused.

"That sounds like fun, Jerry. I'd like that."

"I want you to be comfortable," Jerry said. "I want everything to be perfect for you."

I choked. For the past year, Jerry had been nothing but sweet and patient with me. He'd never once looked at another girl while we were out together. When I met his friends they did nothing more than shake my hand. Not one of them had ever put their hand up my skirt.

Jerry was concerned with my food intake and my comfort. He'd never fuck a girl up against a wall right after making love to me. Jerry would never fuck me to begin with. He wanted to make love to me tomorrow night. In a sense, it would be my first time. I hadn't made love with Hawk or Eagle or Crow, or even Owl. They'd all fucked me.

"Eleanor? Ellie? Is everything okay? Do you still wanna go?"

"Yeah, Jerry. I do wanna go with you."

WE PULLED up at a cabin in the woods. It was more like a cottage with a sloping roof made of logs and a porch with a swing. Inside, Jerry had laid out purple asters. Asters were a daisy-like flower that were a favorite of both bees and butterflies. A peek in the bedroom showed candles waiting to be lit. It was the perfect setting for a romantic weekend.

"Hungry?" Jerry came up behind me. He put his hand at the small of my back. It rested there lightly, without any sensual weight.

I wasn't hungry, but I followed Jerry and sat down at the table. I ate the truffle-covered scallops he'd had prepared for us. We chatted about his schoolwork. He asked questions about mine. Before I knew it, the sun had gone down.

Jerry got up to put the dishes away. "You wanna take a shower?"

"Why?"

He shrugged. "We've been traveling all day. Just thought you might want to be fresh. I'll go in after you."

I fidgeted in my dry underwear. Eagle had three pairs of dirty, soiled panties of mine but Jerry wanted me to come to him clean. Well, that was probably what normal boys wanted; clean girls with clean panties. I went to the shower.

I undressed and looked at myself in the mirror. My nipples were soft, not tight points like Crow liked. There was no abundance of wetness between my legs like Eagle insisted on. I soaped up, dried off, and then went into the bedroom to wait for Jerry.

He came in ten minutes later. He paused in the doorway, mouth agape.

"What's wrong?"

"N-nothing," he stammered. "I just didn't expect..." He waved his hand in the vague direction of my body.

I looked down at myself, still not understanding the problem.

"I thought you'd wear some sexy lingerie," he stammered. "Or underwear, or something."

I lay naked on the bed. It hadn't occurred to me to wear any lingerie for him to take off. For a second a thrill went through my cunt and a trickle of wetness made me ready. Was Jerry going to punish me for not offering him my panties? I felt myself flush at the prospect of a vibrator stuffed in my aching pussy.

Jerry turned away from me. He reached out and turned the lights out. Now, cast in darkness, I felt him approach.

"You wanna get under the covers?" he asked.

It wasn't really a question. He was already pulling back the comforter and sheets. I scooted over and lay down. For a second, I thought we were going to actually go to sleep. But then he awkwardly mounted me. He politely nudged my knees open. I spread for him. I felt him grope around between us for the waistband of his pants. His fingers brushed my core. He inhaled sharply.

"You okay, Jerry?"

"Yeah, yeah. I'm good. You okay?"

"Mmh hmm. Yeah."

He leaned in and put his lips on mine. I realized this was the first time he'd kissed me since he'd picked me up this afternoon. His lips felt stiff, cold.

How had I thought he was passionate before? Before, Hawk.

Thoughts of Hawk putting his mouth on me, tracing his tongue around my mouth, down my neck, invaded my conscious mind. Hawk grabbing the back of my head with his big hand and directing me where he wanted me to go. Hawk watching me with those big eyes that soaked up my pleasure, took it in, and reflected it back at me like it was his own.

"Ohhh," Jerry groaned.

"You okay, Jerry?"

"Yeah," he panted. He looked up at me with a goofy grin. "Was it good for you, too?"

"Pardon?"

"I didn't hurt you, did I?"

My eyes adjusted to the dark. I looked down to see his flaccid penis withdrawing from me, shrinking in the used condom. I hadn't even felt him go in.

TWENTY-ONE

When I left the lab it was late in the evening. The sun had set and there was nothing to guide me back to my dorm but the campus blue lights. Playing hooky last week, and having my head elsewhere the days before, had cost me time on my final projects. I'd been putting in late nights for the past few days.

"You shouldn't be out walking by yourself, sweet meat. Never know when a predator might be lurking in the dark. A sweet little morsel like you would be too hard to resist scooping up and carrying away."

I stopped in my tracks at the sound of that deep voice. He was on me before I turned around. His torso brushed up against my backside. His nose sank into my hair.

I stepped out of his reach and turned. "What are you doing here, Hawk?"

Hawk narrowed his eyes at my retreat but didn't close the distance.

"Shouldn't you be breaking the speed limit or fucking some girl on the hood of a car?"

He grinned. "That sounds like fun. I'm parked just over there if you wanna ride. Or a seat on my hood."

I swallowed. "No, thank you."

"Always so fucking polite."

"Well, there's a lot of naughty girls on this campus, one's who'll suit your tastes better than me. I'm sure you'll find what you're looking for." I turned to leave.

Hawk grabbed my hand. "I came looking for you, Ellie. I want you."

I tried to take my hand from him. He wouldn't let go. He intertwined his fingers with mine.

"I can't..." I looked at his hand, wondering who else those fingers had fondled in the days since I last saw him. "I can't..."

Hawk brought me into his chest. "Shh, baby. Let me hold you, Ellie."

I didn't struggle. Not with him. I stopped

fighting myself, too. I relaxed in his arms. God, I'd missed the smell of him, the feel of him.

He stroked my hair. Planted light kisses on my brow. He tilted my chin up. I looked into his eyes and he looked into mine. I saw sadness reflected back at me.

"Ride with me?" he said.

I hesitated.

"Just a ride, Ellie. I want to show you something. Then I'll bring you back home. I promise."

I allowed myself to be led to his car. He folded my palm into his. Somewhere between the pavement and the passenger door, our fingers intertwined.

Hawk handed me into the passenger seat, then rounded the car to climb into the driver's side. He put the key into the ignition and the engine roared to life, along with my dormant core. My clit perked up, eager for a joy ride. We took off.

Hawk was silent for many miles. He sped down the highway, the miles falling away like the days that had spread between us. He reached his hand over to my thigh. Before it settled on my leg, he paused in mid air. He clenched his fist and put it back on the steering wheel.

We pulled into a residential neighborhood. It

was a gated community. Hawk punched in a code and the gates opened. The guard at the gate nodded at Hawk and leaned back in his seat as we drove past the guard shack.

We drove through the McMansions with pricey cars in the garages and pools in the backyards. They were beautiful homes. The type of homes I'd always dreamed of having with my husband and two kids. We pulled up to a curb, and Hawk put the car in park.

"Where are we, Hawk?"

He turned from looking out the window at the house up on the hill in front of us. "Home."

I looked up at the house. "Whose home?"

"This is where I grew up. My father's a lawyer. Worked sixty hours a week since I was a kid, but he has a strict weekends-off policy. Always came to my soccer games and school functions. My mother was a stay-at-home mom. She was on the PTA and drove us to all our after school activities. I've got a sister. She's an Art major in college. My parents are still married -happily."

I looked up at the house again. It was the life I wanted, the life I'd planned to have with Jerry. The mailbox at the end of the drive had a flag of red, white, and green. The name "Hernandez" was written in bold black on the side of the mailbox.

Hawk turned to me. "I'm not some broken man who's got mommy issues. My father wasn't absent or abusive. I didn't have a rough start. My parents didn't spoil me into thinking I could get whatever I wanted."

He paused, staring into my eyes, searching for understanding. "I fuck who I want to, when I want to, because I want to. I don't need somebody to fix me. This is who I am. This is who I choose to be. I'm not broken, Ellie."

I would be lying if I hadn't assumed exactly what he was disproving. That he'd been abandoned. That he had trust issues. That he didn't know what commitment looked like and I just had to show him. That he'd be so grateful that he'd give up all the other girls and be mine and only mine forever.

Hawk looked me right in the eye. He leaned back so I could get a good glimpse of his picture-perfect upbringing. Then he leaned forward so I could see the earnestness in his face. So that I could see that what he told me about himself was all true; his lived past and his chosen future.

"I'm sorry," he said. "I was wrong to fuck that girl the way I did. I did it to get at you."

"To get at me?"

"You..." He stopped, shook his head, and sighed.

I felt him searching, struggling for words. I wanted to reach out to him, but I stayed my hand.

Hawk tried again. "Ellie I'm never gonna be monogamous. It's just not how I'm built. But I can't stop thinking about... fucking you. I've fucked at least five girls since the last time I saw you. And after I've pulled out of every one of them, I've wanted to come find you and fuck you."

He leaned into the driver's door. He looked at my lips as he ran his thumb back and forth across his own lips. "I don't know what you did to me," he continued. "I've never slept with a woman. Like actually slept in a bed. I don't remember the last time I fucked a woman in a bed. When Eagle caught us together in the morning..." He shrugged. "That girl I fucked in front of you, that was just stupid guy shit. It was childish and I should've handled my shit like a man and not taken it out on you. I'm sorry for that. I will never do disrespectful shit like that to you again."

"I don't understand what you're asking me, Hawk?" I thought about Shakira and Owl and the blurry lines of their relationship. I wanted a clear definition of what was going on between us. "Are you asking me to be a piece of tail for the Watchers Crew? Are you asking me to be your personal fuck buddy?"

I swallowed, but the hope rose in my chest as I put voice to my heart's desire. "Are you asking me to be...your girlfriend?"

Hawk rolled his eyes at the last statement and my heart sank. I felt so stupid, so childish, so naive.

"I fucked my boyfriend," I said.

His face turned from an eye roll to a glare of displeasure. It reminded me of Eagle's glare when I'd shown up without panties. "Who's your boyfriend?"

"It's not like you know him."

Hawk's jaw tensed as though that was exactly his point.

I flustered in my seat. "So you can fuck other girls, but I can't fuck other boys."

Hawk's eyes narrowed on me. "You didn't like it." It was a statement of fact, not a point of inquiry.

I reared back, but I said nothing. I would not give him the satisfaction.

"If this *boy friend*," he made sure to separate the two words, "did right by you, you wouldn't be in this car with me."

"You're a hypocrite." I looked out the window at his childhood home. All the lights were off inside.

"Am I? I like knowing that who ever is fucking you is gonna take care of you. That they're gonna send that sweet pussy of yours into convulsions. I make you come. Hard. Every time. My boys'll do the same. This boyfriend -what the fuck is his name?"

"Jeremiah."

"Jere-fucking-miah. If he doesn't know how to get you off then he doesn't deserve to get between your legs."

"And you get to get other girls off? Any girl you want, any time you want, any way and place you want? And I'm just supposed to wait around for you? Let your boys fuck me while I wait for you?"

Hawk stared at me, his jaw tense. He looked into my eyes and slowly his chest deflated like a balloon. "I'm not gonna lie to you, Ellie. I want you. Bad. But I'm not gonna pretend to be someone I'm not. If that's what you want, the monogamy and the marriage and..." He tilted his head to indicate his parents' home. "If that's part of your plan, then I am not the man for you."

I didn't respond.

"I'll take you home."

He started the car. The engine called to my core. My clit reared up, but my heart was too busy aching to take notice.

TWENTY-TWO

We drove in silence. Hawk kept the car just under the speed limit all the way home. He pulled up to my dorm and put the car in park. We sat there under the street light for long moments in silence.

Finally, he got out of the driver's side. I closed my eyes and exhaled the breath I'd been holding all the way home. When he reached for the door handle I panicked. I nearly reached out my hand to hold the door shut so I could stay in his world a little while longer.

My hands stayed in my lap and he pulled the door open. He offered me his hand. I took it. Those same sparks from the first night we met zipped throughout my body.

Hawk stared in my eyes. He leaned against me

for a moment, my ass against the steel of his car. It all felt so familiar. I wanted to lift my legs around his hips. But he took my hand and pulled me away from the car. He laced his fingers with mine as we walked to my dorm room.

We paused at my door. He looked down at our entwined hands as though he didn't know how that happened. Slowly, he unraveled his fingers from mine. Before our finger pads separated I clenched his fingers back to mine. We stood there leaning against each other.

"I know, baby," he said. "I'm aching for it, too."

We stared at each other. I knew exactly what he was thinking. Maybe, just one more time?

I unlocked the door. I was confronted with the wall I'd been staring at for the last few days. The wall I kept imagining him fucking another girl against. I came inside, stepped out of my panties, and put my face against the wall.

I heard him sigh. But he came up behind me. "Is this what you want, baby?"

"Please."

It felt like forever before he was inside me. He didn't ram into me like he did her. I pushed my hips back into him, hard enough to shove the memory of him fucking her out of my mind. He caught my hips and held me still.

"Behave," he said.

"Fuck me," I said. "Harder."

Hawk put his hands on my waist to settle me down. "I'm going to fuck you the way you need to be fucked. I'm going to fuck you the way I need to fuck you. I'm not going to fuck you like some random piece of meat whose name I don't even remember. Okay, Eleanor?"

I shut my eyes to keep the tears from falling. That should not have been the most romantic thing anyone had ever said to me, but it was. When had I become so fucked up?

"Now, be a good girl or I'll take my dick out of your pussy and put it in your mouth."

That sounded delightful. I rammed back into him. He pulled out of me. I felt myself being lifted off the floor and thrown onto the bed.

Hawk was on me before I was oriented. He pulled off my skirt, ripped open my blouse. His eyes were crazy, hungry. My heart pounded against my chest, causing my nipples to ache with each beat. I spread my legs wide for him.

Hawk lost his pants. He crawled up my body

and straddled my shoulders. Then shoved his dick into my face. "Open."

He put it in my mouth, deep, deeper, until I gagged. He withdrew a bit, but by no means half way. He filled me up. I had to breathe through my nose. He pushed back in, all the way.

Hawk fucked my face while he fingered my clit. Lightly. Not enough to give me the friction I needed. My arms were trapped by his thighs. My head was impaled on his cock. I could do nothing to protest. I was completely at his mercy.

He pulled out. I gasped in a deep breath and was airborne again. He pulled me on top of him. Once he was on his back and I was over his hips, he impaled my pussy down onto his cock. He showed me how to move my hips up and down with a tilting motion at the end. Then he put his hands behind his back and just stared up at me.

"Make yourself come, Ellie. If you're not gonna be with me I want to know that you know how to get yourself off on another guy's cock."

I didn't want to think about another guy's cock. Not with him inside me. I didn't want his cock to leave me.

I worked my hips over top of him. There was no mistaking him inside of me. This man had invaded me. This man was what I'd been missing. This man was what I wanted.

"Move your hips in a circle," he commanded.

I did as Hawk told me. My breath tripped each time I circled to the front and his huge dick hit that delicious spot at the front of my pussy.

"I want you to squeeze your pussy every time you come down, like you're trying to hold your piss."

The first time I clenched, I nearly exploded. I had to stop moving to catch my breath. Hawk waited patiently as I tried again, to the same result. I couldn't go fast or I'd break apart. I didn't want this to end any time soon. And so I went slow.

I made the circles with my hips. I clenched my pussy when I got to the front. The slow rate only lasted for three strokes, and then my hips took over my mind.

I fucked him fast and hard. Gone was the perfectly rounded circular movements. Gone was the slow pussy squeeze. My hips jerked in every direction. The muscles inside my pussy clenched on their own. My orgasm built quickly and brought me down in a crushing tidal wave of pleasure.

Hawk caught me when I fell. He stroked my back until the shaking subsided. Then he put me on my side. Lying face to face with him he fucked me slowly, deeply. Both his dick and his tongue buried deep inside, neither leaving me.

We fell asleep like that. On our sides. Arms and legs wrapped around each other. His dick still buried inside me. His mouth still pressed against mine.

In the morning, when I woke, all traces of him were gone.

TWENTY-THREE

The posted speed limit on the highway was sixty miles per hour. Jerry drove in the slow lane at a constant forty-five miles per hour. I pressed my ass into the cloth-covered passenger seat and got no vibration. There was no friction from the rubber hitting the road, no moisture seeping out of my pussy at high velocities. I was bone dry and bored.

Jerry reached over and patted my knee. The gesture reminded me of a mall Santa patting my knee at eight-years-old after I told him I wanted a butterfly net for Christmas. I'd been a good girl that year, and I'd gotten my Christmas wish. I'd been a naughty girl over the past week and I was getting a lump of coal in my panties.

I looked out the car window and sighed. The

scenery wasn't a blur like it had been when Hawk sped down the highway with me in the passenger seat of his Charger. Rolling along in Jerry's Prius everything was crystal clear to me.

Finals were a week away. The rest of my life was right around the corner. Coming at me from the distance was the life I'd always planned: a modest career, a good marriage, and a happy family.

I shut my eyes and leaned my forehead against the car window. When I opened them again we were passing the exit of where the street race had taken place nearly two weeks ago. The site didn't look as menacing in the light of the day as it had that night. Or maybe I had just changed so much since that short time.

We drove through a residential neighborhood. Jerry pointed out some houses to me. I stared vacantly at their flat tops and even lawns. I watched kids playing in the front yard.

There was one house with a vibrant butterfly garden on the side of the yard. A little girl in pigtails ran around the yard with a butterfly net, trying to catch one. She laughed as they eluded her. Her mother yelled from the porch swing for her to be careful, and not to get her sundress dirty. The little girl paid no heed. She leaped for a butterfly... and missed. She came down on her knee. When she rose, the cloth of her white sundress was muddy brown.

"You like that one?"

I knew Jerry was talking about the two-story house and not the daring little girl. I doubt he'd even seen the series of events; the girl reaching up high for something beyond her grasp, and then falling flat on her face.

I saw the mother's face as she looked displeased and disappointed at the state her daughter was in. For her part, the little girl got up from the ground. She brushed herself off, picked up her net, and leaped after another butterfly.

"Yeah, I like it," I said, not taking my eyes off the little girl who finally managed to catch a butterfly in her net.

Jerry pulled up to a park a few blocks away from the residential neighborhood. He set out a picnic blanket and an assortment of foods. For a second, I was afraid there would be truffles in my turkey sandwich or some other sort of aphrodisiac in the salad. I was getting the impression that Jerry intended this date to last into the night.

"Last weekend was amazing," he said.

We hadn't seen each other since then. We both had a ton of work to do for finals and had only texted or left voice messages after missing each other's calls. I'd been missing Jerry's calls on purpose. Though I didn't think I would be seeing Hawk or any of the other Watchers again, I wasn't sure if I wanted to see Jerry again.

I knew this would be an awkward conversation. I'd been gearing up for it for days. It was now or never. I opened my mouth to speak, but lost my nerve at the last minute. I took a bite of my sandwich and made a noncommittal grunt at Jerry's statement.

My focus turned to the delicious sandwich in my mouth. Jerry had made a turkey on rye sandwich with honey mustard. It was his favorite sandwich. I had never tried honey mustard before dating him. Now, I put it on everything. I wondered if Jerry hadn't have introduced me to the condiment if I would have liked it with another person -I mean, another sandwich?

"I liked waking up next to you," Jerry continued as I devoured the food he'd prepared.

The night we'd spent together, he'd fallen asleep barely two minutes after disposing of the condom. I'd gotten out of bed and wandered around for hours, too restless and unsatisfied to find sleep. I'd sat out in the night air on the deck, under the stars. I'd listened to the sounds of the night. Crickets chirping out late night booty calls. Insects rustling under leaves. An owl hooting from far away.

I became transfixed by the sound of the owl. I'd parted my thighs and masturbated to the sound of the bird's song. I'd been certain that it was watching me from a tree along with other birds of the night. The sounds of my cries of release mingled with the sounds of the night. It was near dawn before I climbed back in the bed with Jerry.

"I'd like to do that more," Jerry said. "Fall asleep beside you. Wake up next to you."

These were words every girl dreamed a guy would say to her. So why wasn't my heart racing? Why wasn't my pussy clenching in anticipation of being with this man who so obviously cared about me and wanted to be with me. Just me. I could probably enjoy sex with him now that Hawk had taught me how to get myself off while riding any cock.

Jerry reached into his pocket and pulled out a box. A small box. My heart did start to pound then.

"Eleanor Russell, would you do me the honor of becoming my wife?"

MY FEET HAD BARELY HIT the pavement before Jerry sped off. He tore out of the dorm parking lot at near seventy miles per hour. It was the first time I'd ever seen him angry. It was also the first time that I'd disagreed with any of his plans.

I watched him disappear down the road. My racing heart settled as he got smaller and smaller in the distance. I felt like I'd just gotten free from a trap that had been slowly ensnaring me.

I couldn't marry him. Not only would it be unfair to him, it would be unfair to me. To the person that I'd become. I was no longer meek and modest Eleanor Russell. I no longer wanted a quiet, secure life that was planned out before I'd even started living it. I'd experienced life in the fast lane, and I was no longer willing to stay on the right side of the road.

I walked towards my building. The sun was setting and the creatures of the night were beginning to make their appearance. I saw worker bees headed away from flowers, likely headed to settle down in the hive for the evening. Inside the hive they'd have to contend with the queen being fawned over by her army of male drones. They'd have to watch as the queen took her pleasure from any male she picked, while they were left in a corner, abstinent.

I looked up to my dorm building. My quiet corner room waited for me, but I couldn't remember what I was hurrying home for? The sounds of an argument captured my attention. Upon further investigation, I noted it was a one-way argument.

In front of the dorm, Shakira had her finger raised and her head waggling before a calm Owl. Owl leaned against his car. His eyes followed her waggling finger. His teeth pulled his lower lip into his mouth as he watched her. Even from this distance I saw his nostrils flaring.

Shakira retracted her finger and loaded it onto her hip. She stared Owl down, jaw tense, lips pursed, eyes narrowed on him, waiting for him to respond. Or to launch an attack.

Owl did neither. He just stared her down, a grin on his face, a light of amusement in his eyes. Shakira squirmed under his intense gaze. I saw the bravado seep out of her squared shoulders.

As though sensing his prey had weakened, Owl attacked. He reached out and yanked her to him. She shoved him back. His grin spread wider. He grabbed her again, spinning her around and shoving her body up against the car. He jammed his knee between her thighs, shoved his big hand into her hair, and crashed into her mouth. Shakira struggled for a few seconds more, but then went slack and pliant against his body.

I stood there watching him kiss her into absolute submission. He turned his head, biting her neck. Her lips parted, and she groaned, shamelessly. Her right leg, which was draped over his thigh, quivered. Owl looked over and caught me staring. He winked at me, and then went back to Shakira's mouth.

There was a small crowd gathered outside. Everyone's eyes were on the two of them. I knew Owl didn't care. From the way Shakira now grabbed his ass, it looked like she was past caring herself. I felt someone grab me from behind.

"There you are, sweet meat." Crow nuzzled his face into my neck. "Where you been? I missed you."

Beneath his crossed arms one of his hands squeezed one of my breasts. The crowd of students that had been watching the brawl, and now the peep show with Shakira and Owl, turned their eyes to me and Crow. I could've gotten away from Crow and his hand.

If I wanted to.

The net of Crow's arms were loose with holes. I could've ducked out and flown away.

If I wanted to.

But Crow's prominent erection felt so good

against my ass. Instead of escaping, I turned in his arms.

"When you gonna come over and play again, Ellie?"

I looked up into his adorable face. His cheekbones were a sculptor's dream. His blond locks would inspire sonnets. And then there was that grin, a grin he'd somehow managed to keep from his time as a precocious child. He pulled me in close, sneaking one of his hands between our bodies. He thumbed my nipple.

"I miss you. You miss me, Ellie?"

I did miss him. I closed my eyes and relaxed into his touch.

"Poor thing," he said. "You need somebody to take care of you. Let me take you home. I'll fuck you good, Ellie. I'll lick those titties raw."

I pressed myself into his hand until his fingers closed around me, eliminating any gap in the net of his arms. I didn't want to be set free. I took his hand and let him carry me away.

TWENTY-FOUR

Crow drove even faster than Hawk. The speed limit was less a suggestion to him than it was a joke. His laughter and glee pumped out of him as he pushed the pedal to the metal. The sound of his jubilation sailed through my ears as the vibrations of the tires skirted over the pavement and worked up to my dormant core. My panties were soaked before we'd gotten to the highway.

It looked like I wasn't the only one affected. In the back seat of the car, Shakira and Owl were diagonal, nearly horizontal. From the rear view mirror, I saw that neither had a seat belt on. Shakira's top was nearly off her shoulders. Owl's thigh pressed rhythmically in between hers. His tongue licked a clear path around her collarbone, up her neck, and behind her ear. Shakira's eyes caught mine in the rear view mirror. A spark of modesty clicked on inside her.

"Wait." She pulled away from Owl.

Owl grabbed her hips and pulled her body flat down onto the back seat; her head met the right side door, her toes met the left side door. Owl grabbed both her wrists in one hand and held them over her head. His other hand disappeared between them.

"Wait for what, Kira?"

Shakira made a strangled sound. Her eyes rolled back in her head. Owl gyrated his hips into hers. His forearm made a sawing motion between them.

"You don't want it, baby?" Owl's voice was silky soft and quiet. He captured Shakira's lips, along with any further protests.

I had to press my thighs together and look away because if she didn't want it, I sure as hell did.

The sounds of Shakira's whimpers filled the car as it sped down the highway. I marveled that Crow didn't offer any running commentary about what was going on in the backseat. But I supposed he knew that Shakira needed some modicum of privacy while she got finger-fucked out in the open. Just like he knew from the moment he saw me walking towards my dorm that I needed a good fuck, too.

The sun dipped into the horizon as we pulled up

to the house. Crow and I got out, giving Owl and Shakira a minute to arrange their clothes and compose themselves in privacy inside the car, which happened to be parked in the middle of the street. From the sounds of the loud base, and the extra cars parked around the house, it was clear that there was another party going on.

"You guys having another orgy?" I asked.

"Orgy?" Crow laughed. "Just some folks over, hanging out."

We went inside to women's clothes littered on the floor all the way down the hall. In the living room, I spotted Eagle on the couch. Two girls sat before him on the wooden coffee table; the same table Crow had laid me out on and fucked my breasts. These two girls were completely nude. Both had their legs spread wide open, their hands behind them holding onto the edge of the table with white knuckles. Their breasts were sharp points, arched into the air. And their heads were thrown back in a cross between ecstasy and agony.

As I took a few more steps into the fray, I saw the reason. The thick end of dildos protruded from both of their cunts. One girl's legs shook as she looked to Eagle with tears in her eyes. Eagle sat back watching the two with a maniacal grin spread across his handsome face. He held two remote controls in his hands. He grinned at the teary-eyed girl shaking his head to and fro. His thumb slowly descended on the dial. Her eyes widened, her chest heaved.

"Oh gawd," she cried before he'd even touched the dial. She threw her head back and braced herself. Eagle turned the dial up and the girl screamed.

The girl beside her watched her companion, transfixed as an orgasm ripped the screaming girl in two. The second girl turned her head to Eagle.

Eagle sat the first controller down in his lap, right next to his obvious erection. He laid the second controller flat in his palm as he eyed the second woman. Her eyes fixed on the controller in his hands. He waited patiently until she looked up at him.

When she did, he raised his eyebrows in silent instruction. The girl leaned back on the table. She spread her thighs wide and arched her back. Eagle smiled his approval. Then he turned the dial up.

The second girl tried to hold on, but it was clearly a losing battle. First her eyes closed. Then her head dipped to her chest. Her legs trembled. Her toes bounced off the floor. Her thighs shook. Her entire body convulsed until she collapsed into the first girl's lap. Her face came right up against the dildo protruding out of the first girl. The second girl eased the dildo out of the first and lapped up her juices.

Eagle grinned at the spectacle, but then he looked up and saw me. There was surprise on his face. He obviously hadn't expected me to come back after Hawk's performance on the work floor with that random girl.

Eagle's surprise quickly changed to hunger. He held up one of the remotes and winked at me. I reached down and raised up my skirt to show him I had in deed brought my tribute. Eagle licked his lips at the sight of my panties, a promise in those dark eyes. Then his attention went back to his first project.

I gathered up my courage and searched out the spot I'd been dreading to see. He was there, in the big chair, with a girl in his lap. She had her hand down his pants. Her hand worked him methodically.

Hawk rubbed the girl's forearm absently. He wasn't looking at her. He stared out the window. His eyes looked vacant. There was a joint in his free hand. He raised it to his lips and took a long pull. He closed his eyes and let out a long puff of smoke. When he opened his eyes again, they landed on me.

We stared at each other for a long moment, neither of us moving.

He blinked first. He removed the girl's hand from his pants. He moved her down to kneel before him on the floor. With his eyes never leaving mine, he guided the girl's head down to his erection. It hadn't been that big a moment ago. Now, it strained the fabric of his pants.

Hawk impaled the girl on his dick and fucked her face. His eyes still on me, holding me there, pleading with me not to look away.

I didn't. I couldn't.

With my gaze on his, his expression finally showed some light. I watched his big, powerful body move. Watched pleasure awaken on his glistening skin.

He pumped into the girl's mouth, contorting her head where he needed it to go. I panted alongside him, aching for him to reach the finish line. I may have mouthed the words "Come on." I wanted him to come, and come hard. He looked like he needed it. More than anything, I wanted him to have it.

And finally, his face broke in absolute pleasure. His eyes shuttered, but never closed completely. They never lost their connection with mine.

After his shudders wore off, he put himself back

in his pants. The girl tried to mount him, but he patted her head like a good puppy and moved past her.

He came to stand before me. "Hey, Ellie."

"Hey, Hawk."

"You got car trouble?"

"No, my car's fine."

He said nothing. He didn't reach out to touch me. He just stared at me.

"I needed to be fucked," I explained. "Crow said he'd fuck me, and I took him up on the offer."

Hawk looked behind me at Crow. I'd forgotten he was there. I turned to look too. Crow had a huge grin on his face, like he'd found the hidden treasure and brought it back home to share.

"He'll fuck you real good, Ellie." Hawk looked at Crow as he said it. It sounded like an order. Hawk gave me one last lingering glance and then he turned and went back to his chair.

TWENTY-FIVE

Crow turned me to face him. His playful smile grew even bigger, if that were possible. He reached for the edges of my blouse and took his time working it up my body and over my head. The whole time I felt Hawk's eyes burning into my back.

Crow bent down and kissed my breasts through the lacy bra. I pressed my knees together as my pussy throbbed in time to his strokes.

"Spread them," Crow said around a mouthful of my right nipple. "Unless you want to piss Eagle off again." Crow ran his teeth over my pebbled nipple and I felt a gushing between my legs. I spread my thighs so that the sweet honey would pool on the cotton crotch for Eagle's collection.

Crow turned his attention to my left breast and

repeated the process. He laved, flicked, and then bit the nipple. My panties were saturated by now and I felt a trickle of warm liquid slide down the skin of my inner thigh.

Crow straightened and took off my bra with one hand. He stuffed the lacy piece of cloth in his back pocket. My underwear budget would explode if I kept hanging out with these guys. Then he bent down and slid my panties off my ass and down my legs. He ducked his head under my skirt, snuck his tongue between my legs, and took a lick for good measure.

"Fuck, do you need it, sweet meat," he said when he emerged from under my skirt. I stepped out of my underwear for him and he tossed the garment to Eagle. It landed on the now vacant wooden coffee table with a wet thwack.

My chest was bare, my pussy too. But I still had on my skirt. Crow lifted me up into the air. I wrapped my legs around his hips on instinct. He made quick work of the condom. Then, beneath my skirt, I felt him aim between my throbbing pussy lips. With one motion he impaled me down on his dick.

"Fuck! Shit! She's a fucking vice."

Off in the distance I heard Hawk and Eagle

chuckle. Crow held me tight while he adjusted to my tightness. I was too eager. I began the cock-gripping technique I'd learned from Hawk.

"Shit! Shit! Fuck a damn duck!" Crow wailed against my chest. Then his tongue found one of my breasts and he suckled. The suckling must've soothed him because he finally began to move.

Slowly.

Shallowly.

I felt desperate for thrusting. I tried to squirm around his hips, but he held me still as he licked my nipples.

"Take her fucking skirt off, Crow." Hawk's growling voice rumbled through me, mirroring my frustration.

"I'll take it off when I'm ready. I want everybody to focus on these gorgeous nipples. I'm making them bloom like roses." Crow laved some more.

I was desperate for thrusting. Just one thrust and I was sure I'd go over. "Please, Crow."

"Fucking fuck her already," growled Hawk. "Or I'll come over there and do it for you."

Crow laughed at both of us. But he also took heed. With one hand he moved my skirt up and over my torso. It fell to the floor to join the pile of discarded clothing. Then he raised my hips up and slammed into me.

I learned I was wrong. That single thrust did not send me over. It woke me up. It put my body on alert that great things were yet to come.

Crow raised me up and slammed into me again. The muscles of my pussy gripped him after the impact, unwilling to let him go, eager for his return. Crow began a brutal rhythm. There was nothing I could do but hold onto him and enjoy the ride.

"Fuck, I love that sound," he said. "That ass slapping sound. Thwack, thwack." He illustrated each sound by pulling my ass down and into his thrusting hips. "You're gonna come hard for me, aren't you sweet meat?"

"Yes, Crow."

But I couldn't come. I wanted to. I stood on the precipice of coming. I looked out over the hill of orgasm ready to descend it. I gripped the edges of the cliff. I couldn't let go. Something was holding me back.

I turned my head and found Hawk watching with wide eyes. The same expression I'd watched him with just moments ago when he'd been getting himself off inside another girl's mouth.

Hawk wanted me to come, wanted it for me,

wanted it for himself. He mouthed the words, "Come on, baby." And just like that, my feet left the cliff, my body went into the air, and I soared.

As my body opened to pleasure, I saw Hawk's face open to relief. As I tumbled down the mountain in a free fall of bliss, I saw a mountain of tension release from Hawk's shoulders. He slumped back into the chair. I slumped into Crow.

"You all better now, Ellie?" Crow whispered in my ear.

I nodded my head while it lay on Crow's chest. "Yes, Crow. I am. I'm all better now."

"Maybe you won't stay away so long next time?"

I opened my eyes to see Hawk rise from his chair. "Don't worry," I said to Crow. "I don't think I'm ever leaving again."

Hawk headed towards us. He strode across the room like he owned the place. He reached for me like he owned me. He grabbed me up and off of Crow. Crow let me go with a wink and a pinch of my nipple.

Hawk carried me across the room and sat back down in his chair with me straddling his hips. My body curled around him, my bare pussy in his lap, my legs tucked on either side of his hips, my chest pressed against his.

Hawk turned my face into the crook of his neck and stroked my hair. His calloused fingers felt like the soft bristles of a baby's brush against my temple. "You're so fucking beautiful when you come, baby. I could watch you get off for hours."

I let my head fall down to his chest where I could hear his heart beating. It beat the same rapid rhythm as mine. I knew I was in trouble. I knew I was never leaving this man. No matter how many girls he fucked in front of me or behind my back. No matter how many nights I spent alone wondering where he was and if he would call. I was all in and there was nothing I could do about it.

It wasn't entirely stupid of me to succumb to this thought. I wasn't way out on a limb with my feelings. There was a connection between Hawk and I.

I knew it was there, deep inside my animal brain; that part of the brain that sought the difference between a haven and danger. I felt it was true in my gut; that part of the belly that knew the difference between lust and disgust.

From the first time he'd touched me, there had been sparks between us. They were here now as he made his chest a haven and caressed my brow. They were present as he ran his large, lustful hand up and down my spine.

This was no normal storybook romance. He'd never pick me up at my door and take me out on a picnic. He'd never spread flowers out or light candles before he fucked me. But I realized that I needed none of that. I wasn't happy with it when I had it.

This, sitting buck naked in a chair in a room full of naked strangers, this made me feel alive and satisfied.

I had left normal behind when I'd spread my legs out in the middle of nowhere in front of Hawk and his crew. I'd left normal behind when I told Jerry I wouldn't marry him. I'd left normal behind when I got into Crow's car this afternoon, eager to get fucked by the friend of the man I was falling hard for. Nothing about my life would be normal again.

It didn't matter. I was all in for this ride, for as long as I could hold on.

TWENTY-SIX

I felt my hips get lifted out from under me. I reluctantly left the nest of Hawk's neck and looked over my shoulder. Eagle was behind me caressing my ass. He gazed down at me. The up tilt of his mouth warned me I was in for a ride.

Eagle put his thumb in his mouth and sucked. He pulled it out with a pop and then ran it over my left ass cheek. I arched back into him. He took that as an invitation to spread my cheeks and place his wet thumb over my anus. I gasped and clenched. Eagle's hand and thumb were trapped between my ass. He ignored my clenching and rubbed light circles around my anus.

At first I was shocked at the intrusion and the dirtiness of it. But after a moment, the circular motion felt hypnotic. My hips pressed back into his thumb. Then he stopped the motion.

I looked behind me to see the reason for the halting. Eagle looked past me to Hawk, his eyebrow raised up in a question. Or was it permission?

I turned my head to Hawk for the answer. Hawk nodded to Eagle. I didn't have a clear understanding of what Hawk had just agreed to on my behalf. I knew I was about to get fucked and that was fine with me.

I assumed Eagle would take me away from Hawk so he could fuck me and maybe rub my ass some more. I would be sad to leave the comfort of Hawk's chest, but I was still horny enough for another go with another Watcher. It didn't look like Hawk was eager to fuck me any time soon. He seemed more eager to watch me get fucked.

Eagle didn't lift me up and take me away from Hawk. The two men arranged me on my knees. Hawk took my arms and wrapped them around his neck so we were faced to face. He grinned at me, running his thumb across my lower lip.

I ached for Hawk's tongue, but I knew better by now. He might kiss me when we were alone together, but he wouldn't do it in front of all of these people. I planted a light kiss on the pad of his thumb, wishing it were his lips. Hawk stared at my lips as though he wished the same. He leaned his head back against the top of the chair and gazed into my eyes.

It should've been awkward; the two of us staring at each other like that. One of us should've blinked or looked away. I did neither. There was so much to see in those deep hazel eyes. He was unguarded in this moment, letting me see past his grin, past his mischief.

I felt something warm and wet on my ass. Actually, on my asshole. I gasped as I realized it was Eagle's tongue. I wanted to tell him to stop that. That it was unsanitary. But it felt so amazingly, incredibly good. I reared back into him instead.

My pussy twitched in time to Eagle's flicks. I tried to press myself back so he would catch my clit. Eagle ignored all of my attempts to redirect his tongue. It stayed firmly, then lightly, on my ass.

Soon he replaced his tongue with a warm and slippery finger. The wetness was thicker than saliva. It was oil. Eagle spread the oil over my anus and then he put his thumb inside me. I made a gurgling sound as he breached my puckered hole.

Once inside, he paused. His eager finger only gave me a moment to adjust to the invasion. Very soon, he began to wiggle his finger around. It should've been uncomfortable. I should've been mortified.

Instead, I learned that there was a whole new set of pleasure nerves at the rear of my body. Stuff never felt this good coming out of there, but it felt amazing going in. Once Eagle sensed I'd figured this out, he inserted another finger.

I gurgled in response to the feeling of fullness up my ass. My head fell onto Hawk's forehead. I opened my eyes and looked down. Hawk smiled up at me, that same proud smile he'd gifted me after he'd taken my virginity and made way for Eagle to take me for a spin.

I felt more oil trickle down my ass. I felt Eagle prepping a third finger to enter me. I swallowed, afraid that I wouldn't be able to take another finger, but more fearful of disappointing Hawk.

Like he could read my mind, Hawk reached over for his joint. He put the thick tip to his lips, took a long pull, and then he blew the smoke in my face.

My first instinct was to look away. Marijuana may have been legalized in the state, but my upbringing still insisted it was a drug.

Hawk grabbed my chin and tugged. "Open," he said.

When this man gave me that command, I had no

choice but to obey. I opened my mouth as he took another pull from his joint. He put his mouth within an inch of mine and blew.

The cloud of smoke hit me like an aphrodisiac. Eagle's fingers slid easily inside me. With another hit of smoke from Hawk, and a few pumps of fingers from Eagle, I shot straight into the stratosphere of cloud nine on an orgasm that began in my ass and spread throughout my entire body.

Eagle withdrew his fingers before my body stopped shaking. Before I knew it, his oiled dick was in my ass. My body shook as the aftershocks of the orgasm clenched around his massive dick in the tight space.

Hawk cupped my chin with his big hands. He slid his thumb across my mouth. "Open," he said, and then blew more smoke into my mouth.

I closed my eyes and took in the smoke and Eagle's dick.

Eagle set a slow rhythm. I didn't expect it to feel good, but it did. Once the thick head of his cock breached the wall of my anus, it was heaven, and the rest of him -well a third of him- slid in easily. I pumped my hips back in time to Eagle's thrusts, certain I could orgasm again.

Hawk smiled at me as though he knew what I

was thinking. There it was again that connection between us. Hawk knew things about me I could've never fathomed about myself. He'd known I'd like this. He'd known I'd like to be fucked in public, by him and his crew. He knew I would never be satisfied by a man like Jerry. And now he patted himself on the back watching his buddy fuck me up the ass.

I wanted to bury my face in Hawk's neck in gratitude for all he'd given me. But I didn't because I knew he wanted to watch the pleasure skate across my face. I leaned my forehead against Hawk's as I took Eagle's dick up my ass. But it appeared that Hawk was more eager to join in than just watch.

Hawk reached to the side and sat his joint down in an ashtray. He came back with a moist towel. Between us, I saw him wipe his dick clean, wiping off the girl who'd blown him before.

My eyes widen. I knew he was about to enter me. Eagle was already a tight fit. Hawk was just as massive. There was simply no way this would work.

"Shh," Hawk hushed at my fears. He ran his hand down the side of my face, tucking away a strand of hair.

I looked into his eyes expecting to see that staunch look of pride he'd given me before each new experience, each challenge to who I was and what I wanted. The look was there, but layered over top of it was one of desire. If I'd been standing, the look of Hawk staring at me with such unguarded hope and desire would've knocked me off my feet.

His hand ended its journey cupping my cheek, asking for my acquiescence. I tilted my head into his hand, eyes locked on his. My eyes reflected the same hope and desire he'd shown me. I nodded my head in affirmation.

Eagle held still inside me while Hawk first put on a condom, and then rearranged my thighs around him. He brought my hips down slowly, eyes never leaving mine.

The head of his cock breached my pussy. My nails dug into his back. Hawk winced and tensed his jaw. I remembered what he'd said about how nails in his back signaled him to be rough. That was the last thing I needed at this point. I let him go and dug my nails into the back of the chair.

Hawk reached up and planted a light kiss on my nose. It was such a silly move that we both grinned at each other. Hawk took advantage of my distraction and squeezed further inside me. I nearly screamed at the tight fit.

"Relax, baby," he said. "I've got you."

I did as Hawk said. I took a deep, relaxing

breath, and I let go. Hawk slipped further inside of me. I knew I would burst wide open at any moment, but I didn't tell them to stop. I trusted them. They'd never done anything to me in the act of sex that had hurt me. Everything each of them had done had brought me to intense pleasure.

Neither man was fully seated inside me when they began thrusting. They did it in tandem; Hawk would thrust when Eagle withdrew, then Eagle would grind his hips into my ass as Hawk pulled out of my pussy. My body received not a second's rest from the onslaught. Within seconds of the sensual seesaw, the inner muscles of my pussy started to clench around Hawk's dick.

Hawk had to hold me tightly as I lost control of my body. I not only lost track of my body, I lost track of space, and time, and my surroundings, and everyone.

I knew that the orgasm had to have stopped because I felt them thrusting again. Slowly, shallowly, gently. It didn't matter. I came again. This time it was the nerve endings in my ass that jerked. I felt Eagle's nails dig into my hips as he tried to hold onto his erection against the onslaught of my orgasm.

And then it began again. They'd thrust, and I'd come. They'd stop moving every time my body tightened. I have no idea how long this lasted. It all felt like one long, deep, hard orgasm to me.

At some point, I felt something warm and eager at my mouth. I opened one eye to see Crow. He was tossing aside a moist towel, likely having just washed off whomever he'd been playing with before coming over to join the three of us. I opened wide for him, suckling at his dick while Eagle pumped his in my ass, and Hawk thrust his up my pussy.

Eagle was the first man to come, his dick jerking inside my ass.

Then Crow came, pulling out so that a good portion of his semen wound up on my breasts and cheeks instead of down my throat.

And finally Hawk came inside my twitching cunt, his forehead pressed against mine, his hands holding my body tight to his.

TWENTY-SEVEN

When I opened my eyes, I saw Eagle and Crow collapsed on the couch with sated grins on their faces. Owl sat in a chair across the room, Shakira in his lap. Her eyes were wide on me. Her chest panted quick breaths. Owl had one hand down the front of her pants, the other forearm held her arms across her chest. I couldn't help myself, I raised an eyebrow at her, the girl who'd called me out for sharing a man and being passed around by his friends.

In response, Shakira shut her eyes, her lips pulled back from her teeth, which clamped down. Her body fell back onto Owl's chest as she shook from her orgasm. Owl caught her, in both his arms and brought her legs into his lap. He stroked her face and planted light kisses on her brow. When she finally opened her eyes, they were full of wonder as they gazed up at him. Fucking continued all around them, but they only had eyes for each other.

I felt like a voyeur watching them and looked away. I turned back to Hawk whose hands stroked my hair, my temple, my lower lip. I pulled back to look at him.

Hawk stared into my eyes in wonderment, the same wonder I'd just witnessed between Owl and Shakira. My heart skipped a few beats.

Hawk brought his face close to mine. I held my breath wondering if he would really do it? Was he really going to kiss me in front of all these people? Halfway to my lips, he stilled. His features clouded over with an annoyed frown.

"Crow, come clean this shit up." Hawk looked up at Crow whose head was already buried in some girl's sized double-D breasts.

Crow had to lean way back from the boobs to catch a view of Hawk's angry face.

"You leave your fucking jizz on my girl again and see if I let you fuck her anymore."

Both Crow and Eagle blinked. The whole room went silent. Dicks that were pumping, tongues that were thrusting, hands that were roaming all paused and stared at Hawk. No, not at Hawk. They were looking at me.

Crow got up, his semi-hard dick swinging between his thighs. He reached for a wet wipe and gently cleaned my face and breasts. He raised his eyebrows at me, as though to say *Good luck with that*, and then he swaggered back over and resettled between the pair of fake boobs.

Eagle stared at me too, the same *good luck* grin on his dark features. Then he crooked his finger at some random girl who came over and sat her naked booty down on his face.

Hawk turned my head left and then right, inspecting my cheeks. When he was satisfied that I was free of any wayward jizz, he leaned in and gave me a gentle kiss on the side of my mouth.

He pulled away and looked into my eyes. Then he pulled me closer and placed his lips directly over mine. He kissed me lightly and carefully, then deeply and thoroughly.

"You good, Ellie?" he asked. "You satisfied?"

I nodded. "Yeah, Hawk. I'm satisfied."

I sat in Hawk's lap for the rest of the night. I watched Eagle and Crow make their way through each girl in the room. Hawk stroked his hand over my arm, over my thigh. He'd plant a kiss on my forehead, then reach down and capture my lips. Once he'd had his fill of my mouth, he'd tuck me back into the crook of his neck and turn his attention back to watch the entertainment.

Other girls approached him, asking for a fuck. Each time he shook his head and told them he was good for the night. He didn't repeat what he'd said to Crow -his claim about me being his girl. But I didn't mind. The public kissing and cuddling was proof enough for me that I was special to him.

At some point Owl materialized before us, Shakira at his side. I noticed Shakira looking around the room. Her gaze wasn't as disgusted as the first night. She peered down at my naked body cuddled in Hawk's arms.

"I'm taking Kira home," Owl said. "You need a ride, Ellie?"

Before I could answer, Hawk spoke for me. "Nah, Ellie's good. She's spending the night."

Owl grinned, that same *good luck* grin that Eagle and Crow had slid my way. He took Shakira by the hand and headed for the door.

Shakira gave me one last glance over her shoulder. Her nod was likely only perceptible to me. It felt something like acceptance, maybe an apology for her harsh words a week ago? I accepted the nod with as warm and welcoming a smile as I could muster, hoping that maybe it might lead to friendship.

Shakira ducked her head uncertainly and slipped out the door behind Owl.

Hawk carried me up the stairs to his bedroom some time later. He laid me down on the mattress and disappeared into the bathroom, reemerging with a cool washcloth. He wiped my body free of the two other men who'd shared me. Then he took off his pants, opened my thighs, and thrust home.

Just like our first night together in his bed, he fucked me slow and deep. His mouth sank into mine as well, his tongue mimicking the motions of his dick. After we both came, hard, clutching at one another, he turned me on my side and tucked me into his chest. We lay there quietly for long moments.

"You're mine," he whispered. "You know that, right."

"Yeah."

I wasn't sure if I spoke out loud, but I knew Hawk heard me. He wrapped his arms around my torso, buried his face in my neck, and threw a leg over mine for good measure. Had I wanted to leave him, there was no way I could've escaped the secure trap of his big body.

"You're mine, too," I said, the possession in my voice pinging off the four walls of the dark room.

I felt a huff of air at my ear. Something like a growl. But it wasn't a rumble of dissent. It sounded like a wild animal settling down into captivity and getting comfortable with the leash around its neck.

It might not have been the L bomb, but I knew it was more than this man had ever planned to give me or any woman. I settled into my captivity knowing these binds would hold us both together for the rest of our lives.

The story is not over!

You saw that Owl is into Shakira.
But Shakira's never had a... how to put this delicately...
Shakira's never had a happy ending.
Poor girl.
Luckily, Owl's just the man for the job.
Read Cruise Control, Book 2 in the Watchers Crew!

Turn the page to check out how their story started...

CRUISE CONTROL SNEAK PEEK!

Chapter One

I KNEW I should've blown my boyfriend this morning, but I had to get to my biology tutor. I'd gotten a series of B's in Biology 101 and it was messing with my 4.0 GPA. So this morning, while he was still sleeping, I decided to blow off giving my man some head and went off to tend to my education instead of tending to his dick.

It was the wrong decision.

There he was, standing in the corner of a bar with his crotch pushed into the hip of some vapid blonde. She giggled and flicked her hair over her bare shoulder as he whispered in her ear. The strobe lights on the dance floor made a sweep over them. The light shone directly into her eyes, and out her ears.

I tried to look away, but I couldn't. The skin around my eyes bunched up like the blinders they put on horses to keep out distractions and keep the animal's attention focused on the direction it needed to go. I stood there and watched Sergio's hand trace over the speed bumps of her breasts. Those hands, which had been in my pussy just last night, took the sharp curve of the blonde's waist and came to rest on the turnpike that was her ass.

The journey was no accident. When I confronted him this time, he couldn't tell me she bumped into his hand. He wouldn't convince me he was just helping her out by reaching for something in her pocket. These were horse blinders over my eyes, not sheep's wool.

I would not accept another lame ass excuse. I would not allow myself to look the other way and pretend I didn't see what was right in front of me. Not this time.

Fuck! Why the hell hadn't I skipped my tutoring session?

I heard my mother's voice in my ear. She always railed that the more educated the woman, the less likely she was to get a husband, especially if she has any color to her skin. The pickings were slim for smart women of color, my momma insisted. When I told her I'd have both, an education and a man, she raised an eyebrow at me and turned back to look out the living room window to perform her one and only task, which was waiting for my father to come home so she could take his shirt and clean off the lipstick stains that weren't her shade of red.

From my position at the bar, I saw the pink lipstick stains on Sergio's collar. I'd picked out that shirt for his birthday last month.

I wasn't even angry any more; I was just tired. Tired of fighting the reality that sooner or later all men cheat. It's just in their DNA. Thanks to my biology lesson, I learned that it's more than human males' DNA. The tendency is in all male animals. My tutor, Ellie, said it's in insects too. Few male species are faithful to their mates.

I knew this. I'd learned it at a young age. I'd had the message reinforced since I began dating in middle school. My cheating-boyfriend-radar had been fine tuned before my junior year of high school.

With Sergio, I'd figured out his phone passcode after our third date, and got access to all his texts, social media, and emails. I'd found him so easily tonight because I'd hacked the GPS in his car (and Momma said my education would get me nowhere with a man). I knew that he'd been cheating since last week. Now, it was just a question of did I want to put in the work to get him back into my bed tonight?

The forecast called for a storm later on tonight. Thunder always woke me up, and I hated waking up in bed by myself. My fingers hovered over the top button of my blouse; ready to release my girls to draw my man back to me. But just then Sergio looked up and caught sight of me. His expression halted my trigger finger. I watched, frozen, as Sergio fit three emotions into two seconds, much like our love life.

His first expression was of shock. His eyes widened as he looked up and recognized that it was me. Then his eyes dropped into guilt. That look sparked hope in my heart.

Maybe this could be salvaged. Maybe I wouldn't have to sleep alone tonight. That blonde was clearly hitting on him. He was just being nice.

He hadn't groped her ass. He'd been shoving the scrap of paper with her number on it back into the back pocket of her jeans. He had to push his fingers into her ass to get it all the way into her pocket because her jeans were so damn tight. It was loud in this place. That's why he leaned down to whisper in her ear; to communicate to her that he had a girlfriend.

But then Sergio's face morphed into a sneer. His head tilted to the side. His mouth opened as though he let out a single, huffing bark of laughter.

The music blared, but I heard that huff of laughter from across the room. More than waking up alone to the sound of thunder, I hated that look of pity my exes got on their faces when it finally clicked for them the depths I went to track them down and try to hold on to them.

I couldn't handle that look, not tonight. I turned my back on my ex and searched desperately for a Plan B. I zeroed in on the first thing I saw with pecs and biceps.

Dark eyes stared back at me through almond-shaped eyelids. Intelligence oozed out of the corners of those long lashes. Generally, I didn't prefer my victims to be smart. I liked them with big dicks and small brains. It made them easier to control when I could simply yank on the biggest parts of their body to get their attention. This guy's dark eyes were so clear I saw my reflection in the dim lighting. It looked as though he'd seen everything that had just gone down and knew what was about to happen next.

"Do you have a girlfriend?" I have no idea why I asked him that question. Maybe because I believed in karma and I didn't want it coming back around on me for what I was about to do.

"No." His voice was quiet, a whisper over his silky tongue, but I heard him clearly. He said that one word with a slight raise of his eyebrow, as though the concept was juvenile, ridiculous.

He was likely a player, had to be with those good looks and easy confidence. He was Asian, but I wasn't down enough with Asian culture to know which country.

His skin had a deep tan to it. His dark hair rested just above his eyebrows in a wave, as though he'd swept it out of his way just a moment ago. It fell back over his eyes as he tilted his head down to survey my body. I could tell that I met his approval when his nostrils flared as they swept over my breasts. He suited perfectly for my plan.

"Good," I said just before I reached up to pull his head down to my mouth.

He didn't jerk back from me in disgust. Neither did he gasp as though surprised by my actions. He didn't open his mouth and try to shove his tongue down my throat. Neither did he open for me as I licked sensually at his lips. He just stood there, letting me lick my tongue futilely. And then, I felt his hand move between us.

My tongue rested on the divot at the middle of his lower lip as my attention focused on the track of his hand. His fingers lightly traced down my side. It was a gentle touch. It skittered the fabric of my blouse, giving only a bit of pressure to the skin beneath. He continued the motion across my belly, and on down to my pubic bone. Before he got those sneaky fingers in between my legs, I gasped and pulled my mouth away from him.

"What do you think you're doing?" I shuffled back half a step, but then I stopped and pressed my thighs together. The areas where his fingers had contacted my skin through the fabric of my clothes all tingled.

"You tried to put your tongue in my mouth." He leaned back against the bar. "I tried to put my hand in your pussy."

I straightened my shoulders with a huff while my pussy buzzed at the sound of its name on this guy's tongue. "I was only kissing you."

"I don't see a difference," he shrugged.

From the corner of my eye, I saw Sergio, my

boyfriend. Strike that- my ex boyfriend. Sergio, my ex boyfriend, was making his way over to us. He fumbled a step as he evidently caught sight of the man standing with me. Sergio's hand went to his chin. He scratched at the pity he'd been about to present to me. That pitiful expression was slowly crumbling away.

"Look," I turned back to the guy at the bar. "I just caught my boyfriend cheating on me."

"Boyfriend?" There went that eyebrow again.

I didn't like the way he said that word with a smirk. Instead of the twenty-year old modern woman I was, I felt he was looking at me as though I had on a poodle skirt and I'd just told him my steady guy offered me a promise ring.

The truth was Sergio had never promised me anything. I'd called him my boyfriend, but he'd never confirmed it by calling me his girlfriend in return. Nor had we exactly said we'd be exclusive to each other, but we had been screwing around for over a month now. Thirty plus days of fucking and blowjobs should imply exclusivity.

The Asian guy looked around the dance floor. "Your man is in here fucking another girl?" His voice was full of interest, as though he would like to see that show.

"No," I grimaced. "He was talking to some girl over in the corner. He just saw me and he's headed this way."

Just like Sergio scratched his chin a second ago, this guy's hand rose and scratched as he considered my words. "He was just *talking* to some girl?"

It wasn't pity on his face, but I still felt like he was speaking to me as though I were a child coming to him with an adolescent's concern, like someone was playing with my Ken doll without my permission.

"Can you just pretend to be here with me?" I said. "Just for a minute, and then I'll leave you alone. Please?"

His calm face studied me. Then his dark eyes flicked over my shoulder. He reached up and wrapped an arm around my waist. "Sure, but only because I like how you beg."

"Kira?"

I stiffened at the sound of Sergio's voice behind me. In front of me, my eyes pleaded with my sexy decoy to be cool. In response, the corner of his sexy mouth ticked up. Decoy man moved his hand from my hip and rested it on my ass. I pursed my lips, but I let it stand and turned around.

Sergio stood there, alone. I saw the blonde

standing in his wake. I placed my hand on the Asian guy's chest. I had to take a moment to enjoy the play of muscles there beneath his soft cotton shirt. I was a sucker for a well-defined chest.

I put on my brightest smile. "Hey Serg, I thought that was you over there. You having a good time?"

Sergio looked between me and the Asian guy, then over his shoulder at the blonde. "Yeah, I'm just hanging out with some friends." He turned back. "I thought we had plans tonight?"

I arranged my face into a theatrical wince. "I didn't think we'd set anything firm. I'm not sure when I'll be home."

My partner in this lie took the hint and pulled me closer to him, nuzzling my ear. "*If* you'll be home," the Asian said in my ear, but loud enough for Sergio to hear.

I giggled like one of those vapid girls that I couldn't stand. "Sorry, Serg. Maybe some other time?"

"Forget it, you cunt. I don't do sloppy seconds."

I saw red. Before I could launch into an attack, my decoy stepped up.

The Asian guy locked his arm around my waist, his fingers dug into my ass. "You're the sloppy one if your girl needs to go out and look for somebody else to satisfy her."

Sergio reared up. He thrust his chest out and bared his teeth. "She's not even worth it. She can't fuck for shit."

Again I was ready to stand up for myself and lay into Sergio, but the Asian guy's hand, which was still on my side, dug into me, commanding me to stay put and quiet.

He tucked me behind him and squared off, planting his feet wide. From over his shoulder I saw the smile on his face, challenging Sergio to make a move. Sergio was bigger than this guy. That didn't seem to bother my decoy. A crowd gathered. A bouncer came over.

Sergio took a step behind the bouncer. "Yeah, you better hold me back. You don't want to mess with me, man."

The bouncer escorted Sergio to the front door. He left me and the Asian guy alone without a second glance.

Once Sergio was out the door, the Asian guy offered me his hand. "Come on."

I put my hand in his and we headed towards the exit. In the dark night's sky, gray storm clouds overran the deep blue. The rumble of thunder could be heard in the distance. I wrapped my arms around myself in the humid air as I thought about the long, sleepless night ahead of me.

"Thank you," I said to my rescuer. "I appreciate your help with that."

He shrugged as though it meant nothing. It probably hadn't. He'd gotten to grope a woman and flex his muscles. Now, he'd go off and fuck one of the many women who had eyed him appreciatively on his way out the door.

"But you know," I said, "you didn't have to try to put your hand up my skirt."

"You tried to put your tongue in my mouth."

"I kissed you. You groped me."

"Yeah, I still don't see the difference," he said. "Do you know how many germs are carried in the human mouth? A woman's pussy is far more hygienic a place for a man to put his tongue than in their mouth. A man's dick is also a more hygienic thing to put into your mouth than someone else's tongue."

Was this guy for real? "So, what? I violated you?"

"Yes. If you'd asked me to kiss you, I would've said no. I don't know you or where your mouth has been. If you'd asked me to eat out your pussy, I would've said yes. Would you like me to eat out your pussy?"

I stumbled down the last step. "No."

"Are you sure? You look like you need a good release after fucking that prick. When's the last time you came?"

"None of your business."

"Would you like to make it my business?"

I couldn't respond. My body was tingling again at all the places where he'd touched me; the left side of my body where his fingers had traced. My hip, my ass, my stomach, and just below my pubic bone.

Sergio was full of shit. I wasn't a bad lay. He never complained before. I always got him off. But it was never the other way around. This guy beside me gave me the feels with my clothes on.

"I'd like to make it my business," said the man who'd made me tingle with a touch. "You put your tongue in my mouth. Let me put mine in your pussy, and then we'll call it even."

From the corner of my eye I saw Sergio putting the blonde into his car. The best way to get over one guy was to get under another. That's how I got over the guy I dated before going out with Sergio. Why mess with tradition?

Plus, this guy was cute. Those dark, intelligent

eyes of his were glazing over in desire for me. I'd got an impression of his size when I'd pressed myself up against him. That thing had to be bigger than his brain. I wouldn't mind leading it around for a bit.

Why not? I sure as hell didn't want to go home alone after that scene. And who knows? He might make an excellent new boyfriend.

"What's your name?" I said.

"You can call me Owl."

"Hi, Owl, I'm Kira."

CHAPTER Two

OWL LED me around back to the parking lot. On the way there he tucked my hand into the crook of his arm, just like they did on those old Masterpiece Theater period movies.

"We're going to fuck, not court." I pulled my arm away. That public display of affection was more than I'd ever received from any other boyfriend.

Owl's chuckle was light as it breezed across the tip of my ear. "Should I push you into the alley, shove up your skirt, and fuck you in front of all these people?" He stopped walking, turned, and faced me. "Would you like that, Kira?"

There were people on the streets, but none in the actual parking lot. I wasn't into public sex, but the way he looked at me, the way he'd said that, my brain -no, my pussy- actually considered it. Too bad he was kidding.

He was kidding, right? We faced off in the middle of the lot. He stared at me, waiting for my answer. My mouth wouldn't work.

But then he grinned. "My car's just over here."

Owl put my arm back into the crook of his elbow and led me over to a red Honda Civic with a black and gold dragon painted on the side. The car was sandwiched in between three other cars that looked like they belonged in the movie *The Fast and the Furious*. There was a black Charger, a green Audi R8, and a gray BMW coupe.

How did I know the make and models? I'd had a lot of boyfriends. All the cars had unique paint jobs, but I didn't get a chance to admire them in the dim street lighting. Owl opened the rear passenger door of the Civic for me.

I turned to him and frowned. "Aren't you taking me home?"

He leaned into me, pressing my body into the

frame of the car. "You shouldn't go home with strange men, Kira. You don't know what they might do to you."

It was smart advice that I'd ignored for a good portion of my adult life. I'd gone home with a ton of strange men. The worst thing to happen to me so far was waking up alone with a sore pussy and aching thighs.

"You told me what you wanted to do to me," I said. "You said you were going to eat me out."

"Baby, I'm going to make a meal out of you. Now, be a good girl and hop in the back seat."

He didn't raise his voice. He hadn't raised his voice at any point during our encounter, not even when he squared off against Sergio. Owl spoke in these quiet, dulcet tones that would lure a child to sleep, or off the wooded path to Grandma's house.

I expected him to challenge me, to try to cajole me. He did neither. He waited silently. His dark eyes dared me to step inside. I could turn around and leave. I didn't think that he would stop me if I tried to go.

I looked again at his firm body, his broad chest. It was going to be nice to curl up into that chest later this night and more nights to come. I ducked into the car.

Once inside I scooted to the opposite door placing my heeled shoes on the floor. Owl crawled in and shut the door. His body took up any remaining space in the cramped back seat.

I reached up and grabbed his neck. In a move that would've made any martial artist proud, Owl's hands snaked out and grabbed my wrists. His fingers entwined with mine and he put them behind my head. The move knocked my breath out, made my heart speed up.

When he spoke it was that soft, calm voice. "What did I say about kissing?"

There was a firmness behind his words that turned my intellectual brain to mush.

"Kissing is a messy business, Kira, and I don't do that with strangers."

I struggled to add meaning to those words. "But you're going to eat me out."

Owl grinned. "Pussy is a delicacy I don't pass up." He reached his hand under my skirt and traced the seam of my g-string. "Ohh," he purred as he traced my bare pubic area. "And it looks like you cleaned up for me."

I wasn't a fan of pubic hair and always kept it shaved off. Actually, I wasn't a fan of guys eating me out either. I'd always offer a different course instead.

"Why don't you turn around so I can give you a little head? As a thank you for helping me out."

"Maybe." Owl rubbed his thumb over my bare pussy lips. "When I'm done."

I failed to stifle my sigh of frustration and turned it into a moan of what I hoped sounded like pleasure. I writhed my hips to encourage him to get on with it. That storm was coming soon. I wanted to be inside, out of the shower, and in bed with him before it broke.

Owl moved aside the fabric that covered my pussy. I held my breath expecting dry friction over my vagina. But instead, his fingers slipped and slid between my folds. To my surprise there was wetness there. My gasp this time wasn't an act.

Owl brought his thumb back from under my skirt. He put it in his mouth and sucked. "Hmmm."

His groan rumbled through me. I watched his tongue flick out of his mouth and over his thick thumb. A throb reverberated through my core. I jerked, shocked at the sensation.

"You just passed my taste test, Kira."

Another throb went through me. This time it rose up my back and reached the top of my spine, straightening my shoulders on the leather of the car seat. It was the nicest thing a guy had said to me in a long time. I think I could really come to like this guy. I reached between us for his dick.

"Let me suck you off," I said. "I give really good head."

Owl smiled at me. "Me, too." He shoved away my hands and disappeared between my thighs.

I sighed again. Hopefully, he took it as a sigh of pleasure. In truth, it was a sigh of irritation.

Owl seemed like the type of guy that actually got girls off instead of bragging about how they made their pussies drip drop. He seemed like the type of guy that was gentleman enough to stay down there until a girl came. I groaned, but not in the good way. It was going to be a long night.

I spread my legs wide for him and settled down to begin my practiced orgasmic performance. I took advantage of his deep growl of pleasure to clear my throat to prepare my vocal cords for the high-pitched soprano I was about to sing for his benefit.

Owl didn't go directly for my clit. He played in the creases of my thighs. I tried to help him by rotating my hips to get him more center. I wanted to get this party started, and over with as quickly as possible. But he used his big hands to maneuver me back into place.

I gave up and called up my to-do list for tomorrow. I needed to get some school supplies to prep for finals, which were coming up soon. I began to compile a detailed list of what to get, and where to get it in my head as Owl nibbled on my left labia.

I couldn't remember if I had a box of notecards or if I needed to get a new box. I moaned again and thrust my pussy absentmindedly into Owl's mouth. I'd just add notecards to the list and if I wound up with two boxes it was cool.

Owl flicked at my clit.

"Oh," I moaned low and long trying to recall which size paper clips I was low on.

He flicked again.

"Oh god, yes." I elongated the *yes* for an entire breath and clenched my thighs around his face. That always got them riled up and ready to plunge into my pussy.

Owl pulled away from me. He rested his chin on my pubic bone and stared up at me. "You in a rush, Kira?"

The question threw me. My shopping list fell to shreds in my head. I forgot which octave I'd left off in my moaning. Owl's eyes were bright, alert. Shouldn't he have only two brain cells in working order right now?

"It just feels so good," I said with the same bright

smile I'd given Sergio twenty minutes ago. "I was almost there."

Owl raised that eyebrow again. "Were you now?"

It was a challenge, like he knew the truth; that I was faking it.

"Yeah," I lied. "What would really help me is if I could put your dick in my mouth. That really turns me on." And it would get him off and put him into a coma by the time I got him back to my place where I could rest easily against his warm body.

"He never got you off, did he?"

Fuck. Owl had more than a few brain cells working. He had complete control of his faculties.

No, Sergio had never gotten me off. No guy had ever gotten me off. Hell, I had never gotten off, period. I'd never experienced an orgasm in my life, but I wasn't about to tell Owl that. He looked like the type of guy who would take that as a challenge and I didn't have time to deal with his male ego. There was a storm coming, and I had a big bed to fill.

"I'm going to take care of you, Kira."

The words sailed into my being and fogged up my brain. My belly clenched and that tingling over my skin started up again. I couldn't help but hope that this one would be The One. That this one would last.

My head cleared when Owl inserted first one than two fingers into my pussy. I realized he was talking about taking care of my orgasm, not taking care of me as a person. Of course that was his goal. He was a guy. He had to prove his manhood, especially now that he knew that Sergio hadn't been man enough for the job. Owl was not going to stop until he got me to come.

I took another deep breath and got my mind ready to give a convincing performance.

Owl stroked his fingers in an upward motion. I breathed a sigh of relief. It was uncomfortable. Discomfort was a familiar thing to me when it came to sex. This I knew how to handle. I moaned again like his two-pronged stabbing was the greatest thing in the world.

"Oh yeah," I moaned. "Right there, baby."

Owl stroked faster.

"That's... that's..." I fell over my words as the motion of his fingers hit a spot. It didn't feel good, per se. It felt... it was hard to describe how it felt.

There was a heaviness building inside me, like I had to pee. I tried to squirm away from him, but he had my hips on lock down. I had to end this now before I embarrassed myself any further.

"Yes, yes." I called on my inner Meg Ryan. "Oh gawd, Owl. Awww." The performance would've won me an Oscar. I slumped back against the seat with a grin on my face.

Owl loomed over me. That same eyebrow rose as he peered down at me with an unconvinced face. My fake panting slowed. My sated grin faltered.

Owl leaned back down between my legs. He placed his fingers back inside me, not all the way, just up to the knuckles. He moved his fingers fast, faster. And then he added his tongue to my clit.

"Owl, what are you ahh..."

I jerked. A tremor started in my leg. The feeling of needing to pee intensified.

"Owl... wait... I'm gonna..."

It felt like my hips were being stacked with bricks of pressure. I bore down into the back seat of the car trying to release it, trying to get away from him. But he didn't stop. He wouldn't stop.

And then my body tensed, like the bricks that were weighing me down suddenly grew fingers. The fingers wrapped around me with that same amount of pressure, but they held me tight in a vice. They pressed into me, deep into me.

I couldn't speak. I couldn't breath. At any moment they were going to rip me apart. And then, I realized, I wanted to be ripped apart. I needed to be torn in two.

As soon as I came to that realization, as soon as my body was about to open up, Owl stopped.

CHAPTER Three

OWL REMOVED his tongue and his fingers from my pussy. My body trembled from the loss. I needed him to finish what he'd started, to break me open, and relieve all that pressure he'd built up inside me.

He pulled back from me and unbuckled his pants. He took out his dick. I'd been right in my estimation of his size. It was an impressive instrument, long and thick with a slight curve. He pulled a condom from his back pocket and tore it open with his teeth. He did all of this slowly, with absolutely no sense of urgency, while I lay writhing beneath him.

I was panting hard, whimpering. My body ached for his fingers to return, for his tongue to lick at my clit again. Had I been about to come?

I didn't want his dick. I didn't want him to pump into me and bang away until he came. I wanted to come. And I half believed that I could.

But I couldn't ask him to go back to what he'd been doing before. I'd already pretended that I'd had my orgasm. And it looked like he knew it had been fake. That grin on his face as he placed the condom tip over his dick looked like he was teasing me.

"Oh, I almost forgot." He removed the unrolled condom from his dick, leaned back against the opposite door, and held his dick out. "Here you go," he said as he stroked the precum around the head. "Is this what you want, Kira? To suck me off?"

No, I wanted his face back between my thighs. I wanted his fingers hitting that spot. But I'd settle for this right now.

I was good at this; sucking dick. That's how I'd kept a man around for the last few years. I'd do this for him now, and maybe tomorrow night I'd get him to finger fuck me again. Maybe tomorrow night I'd have my first real orgasm with this quiet man with the intense eyes and magic hands.

I moved to get up. My knees wobbled as I put weight on them. My pussy felt like a weight hung from its center. I had to brace myself on the back of the driver's seat. Owl caught my upper body, a smirk on his face as he guided me down and onto his dick.

I gave him one last glance before I sank down into his lap. Now, it was my turn to smirk at him. He didn't know what he was in for.

I took hold of the base of his cock, holding it firm as I licked at the head. He was long with a nice girth. I'd seen my fair share of penises. It was easy to lead around the big, thick ones. But I preferred the small, skinny ones to be inside of me. They were no bother when they were in there. The thick ones always left me sore the next day.

I had planned to get Owl off quick, but I liked the feel of him on my lips, the taste of him on my tongue. Most girls I knew didn't like giving head. Most of the time I sided with them and their distaste of the act. It was a chore, but a necessary chore for a girl like me who wanted to keep a man around while she went off to the library to study. Every once in a while I found myself enjoying the chore.

I was enjoying myself with Owl. With the tip of my tongue I played with the veins along his dick. I licked at his balls, enjoying the shifting texture of his sack. He reached his hand down. I expected him to guide me fully onto his dick. But he didn't. He ran his fingers through my hair, gently, like a caress. I shuddered as they traced the cone of my ear.

I got down to business. I put him in my mouth, working my tongue around his shaft. I relaxed my throat muscles and took him in deep, all the way to the back of my throat. There was still another inch or two of him that I couldn't fit.

Damn. He was the biggest dick I'd yet to encounter. I pulled out my whole bag of tricks.

I leaned my torso down, putting my ass in the air for him to admire.

I kissed at his length, using my words to compliment his impressive instrument.

I took him back in, sucking hard and making a pop when I withdrew.

I deep throated him, slobbering all over his length in the process.

Throughout my performance, Owl watched me with half lidded eyes. He didn't pump into my mouth. He didn't grab my ears or the back of my neck to keep me down there. He didn't impale himself up and into me. He relaxed back and let me do my thing.

His eyes never left me. That same soft smile on his face. His breathing was even. Long moments passed like this; him relaxed and me hard at work.

What the hell was happening? I'd always gotten guys off in less than five minutes -without fail. My jaw was becoming tired. I'd never jerked a guy off for this long without a result.

"Kira?" He reached down and lifted my mouth off his dick. "I want to fuck you now."

The head of his thick, long dick bounced off my chin. I looked at it. It curved in that same angle that his fingers did when they were inside me.

Maybe...?

Would I...?

Could I...?

I was throbbing between my thighs, aching to be filled by something. I'd been so close. Maybe he could get me there? Maybe he could get me to come?

I crawled over top of him. He slid his pants further down his thighs and rolled the condom on. He pushed my skirt up. He didn't bother removing my underwear, just kept the panties pushed to the side. He slowly impaled himself up and into me, allowing me to feel every inch of him. It should've hurt, but it was a welcome intrusion to my throbbing pussy.

Once he was all the way in, he stopped. He sat up with my knees spread wide over his thighs. He reached out and undid my shirt. With the buttons free, he pulled the garment down behind my back trapping my upper arms in the sleeves.

I couldn't move my upper body with my forearms trapped like that. I couldn't move my thighs with him inside of me. I was at his complete mercy.

He put us eye to eye and then he fucked up and into me. Not hard, but firm enough for me to feel every inch of him. Not slow, but fast enough to keep me panting. The moans came out of me unbidden. I felt that sweet pressure return. My eyes closed and my head lolled back.

"Kira."

I tried to give him my attention, but the pressure was collecting all around me.

"Kira, I don't want you to come."

His words made no sense. I must've imagined them in all of my haze.

I heard people coming around us, filling in the parking lot. Someone turned on an engine and music blared. I should care. I should tell Owl to stop, that someone might come close and see what we were doing, what he was doing to me. But I couldn't give them that much of my mind. It was all wrapped around Owl's dick and the magic it was working inside of me.

"Kira, you're gonna wait for me to come, and I'm not ready."

That was definitely Owl's calm voice, the calm tinged with the firm command that had rankled me earlier. I'd listened to that commanding tone before, but I would not listen to it now.

Like hell I would wait.

I was so close. I'd never been this close in my entire life. I needed this. My thighs trembled. With one more thrust I'd be over this barrier.

Owl stopped and withdrew from me.

I felt like the world had been pulled out from under me. I felt like I'd been shoved off a cliff and was left flailing in the air, waiting for the impact of the ground to rend me into pieces. I felt like I'd been surfing on the tallest wave and crashed down into a wall of water that left my body stinging.

I could've screamed. Maybe I did scream. I couldn't move my arms, which were trapped in my blouse. I couldn't move my legs, which he had spread wide over his thighs.

I opened my eyes and glared at him.

Owl stared at me. His face transformed from calm amusement to displeasure. "I told you not to come, Kira."

The anger seeped from me as I looked at the

displeased lines that gathered at the edges of his eyes. "I...I didn't," I panted.

Owl traced the lines of my lips, my chin. I leaned into his touch like an eager kitten aching to be petted. A small smile broke over his mouth as he watched me. "But you want to. Don't you, Kira?"

What the fuck kind of mind games was this guy playing? I was frustrated and horny. I was on the verge of something I'd never experienced, something I thought other girls exaggerated about. And this guy was holding it from me, dangling it over my head while he laughed at me.

"Tell me you wanna come, Kira."

"What?"

"Beg me for it."

"You're an asshole."

Owl smiled. He dipped down and bit my breast through the lace of my bra.

I gasped. My legs shook. Something tightened in my core, but as it tightened I felt a fresh flush of wetness leak out of me.

"Mmm," Owl groaned. "Say it, and I'll give it to you." He reached down between us. He rubbed his thumb over my clit and then around my pussy lips where I'd dripped all over him. He stuck two fingers just inside my channel, coming just to the edge of that sweet spot.

He leaned back against the car seat. He stuck his fingers in his mouth, the fingers he'd just had in my wet, dripping pussy. I watched his tongue flicking over his digits. The throbbing increased in my pussy. I couldn't rub my thighs together because he had them spread wide. I couldn't touch myself because my hands were trapped. I would go out of my mind if I didn't get relief soon.

"Please, Owl. I'm begging you. This is me begging you."

Owl smiled. He grabbed his dick and thrust deep into me.

CHAPTER FOUR

BUT OWL DIDN'T LET me come right away. He continued to toy with me, thrusting fast and hard, and then slow and shallow.

"Fuck, you need it, baby. Don't you?"

"Please," I whimpered, no longer shamed at my neediness. I was already supplicating myself in his lap. My head bowed in reverence to the mastery he had over my pussy.

"Okay, baby. You wanna come?"

"Yes, please."

"Come for me, Kira."

And that was all it took.

It was better than I'd ever hoped it could be. It felt like I was in the movies. In those action scenes where time slows down.

I held on as Owl continued to stroke into me, slowly. I felt my body open up, like someone unlocking a door. I saw the key turning in the lock as the head of his penis pushed once more past my pussy lips. I heard the click as his dick filled me from my entrance all the way through to what felt like my belly.

That's when I knew I was going to come. But that wasn't the end. No, there was so much more.

Before my pussy clenched around him, his penis traveled back down the way it came, hitting every spot again. My heartbeat dropped; the rhythm slowed, and the beating descended into my pussy. I watched the door opening, heard it creaking wider and wider. I knew without a doubt that any minute it would be flung wide open and I would be knocked back.

It was an out of body experience. I sat high above myself, watching it all take place, suspended in the live animation of it all. And he was right there with me. Through the slowing of time, the turning of the lock, the opening of the door. At the exact moment that the door swung open, Owl grinned at me like he knew it was about to happen... right... now...

My body stiffened. My pussy seized and clamped around his thick cock, which was buried deep inside of me, as deep as he could push into me. The muscles inside my pussy felt like they contracted for an hour, and during that long wait for them to release I couldn't breathe . I couldn't move. I couldn't even think. I only saw him, grinning wide like a proud lion, eyes opened wide like his namesake bird, taking it all in like it was beautiful, like I was beautiful.

I sighed and my body released. The sounds I made when I came were nothing like what I'd heard Meg Ryan doing in that movie. It was nothing like the canned cries of real porn stars. The sounds that came out of me were deep, guttural, helpless. Joyful.

When I stopped jerking, I collapsed against Owl, my face buried in the center of his chest

Owl pet my hair. "Good girl. That's better, isn't it?"

The self-preservation part of me knew I needed to get up off this dude and get as far away from him as possible. The amount of power and control he'd just exuded over not just my body, but my head as well, was more than any person ought to have over another human being. Plus, it was clear that he liked to play games. I didn't need another guy who would jerk me around.

But my body clamped itself around him. It wrapped itself around him and wouldn't let go. My arms, which had been freed sometime during or after my orgasm, were clasped around his biceps. My knees pressed into his thighs. He was still inside of me, not as hard as when I clenched around him during my orgasm, but still erect enough to stay inside me. My mind may have been saying run, but my body had other intentions.

"Hey Owl, you done in there?" Along with the voice from outside the car came a rap at the window.

The windows were tinted, but I could make out a large shadow. I jerked away from Owl, reaching for the ends of my shirt to cover myself. As I reached I felt my hips rooted to something, Owl's semi hard dick still buried deep inside of me.

"Relax," he said to me leaning back against the seat, making no move to remove his dick from my pussy. "It's just my boys."

His boys? Were they out there the whole time? We're they watching? I squirmed on top of him, trying to free myself from the anchor of his dick.

"You need some help in there?" said one of his boys.

Owl raised an eyebrow at me at the question. Then he chuckled at my reaction. He reached out his hands and freed me from his dick. "No we're good," he yelled to who ever was outside the car.

Owl's dick lay prone on his ripped lower abs. The purple condom glistened in the moon's light leaving tracks of my pussy juice at the edge of his navel. He patiently unfolded my arms from my breasts. He pulled my blouse back up and over my arms. He took his time fastening each button.

He reached between us and pulled the fabric of my underwear back over my pussy and straightened my skirt back over my still quivering legs. Then he motioned for me to climb off him so he could straighten himself out.

I sat huddled against the door watching him dispose of the condom and put his dick away with those magic fingers. My pussy, which felt like it had been opened for the first time, still sang his praises in a throbbing rhythm. Once Owl had himself put back together, he got out of the rear passenger door. He reached back in and held his hand out for me like a gentleman.

I stepped out of the car on shaky legs. Owl wrapped his other hand around my waist and held me steady.

"Fuck man, I see why you didn't want to share."

I looked over Owl's shoulder to see a bear of a man grinning down at me like I was a tasty morsel he wanted to pick his teeth with. He was flanked by two other men. Though not as big as him, they were both forces to be reckoned with. One was blond with the face of an angel, which let me know there had to be a devil hidden behind his dimpled cheeks. The other was a brother with a shiny, bald head.

"I'm gonna take her home," Owl said, opening the front passenger door and handing me inside. "I'll see you guys back at the house." He shut the door and went around to the driver's side. He started the car, and we were off.

"Did you have a good time?" His eyes were on the road as he asked. He asked the question as though we were talking about the weather.

"Were your friends there the whole time we were...?"

Owl shrugged. "I don't know? Probably not. They would've knocked on the window earlier and asked if you wanted them to join in."

"Join in?"

"Yeah." He didn't elaborate.

"So you guys do stuff like that? Share women?"

Owl turned to me with a smile. "Hey kettle, don't call me black when you just went from your boyfriend's limp dick to the back seat of my car."

"My ex-boyfriend who was cheating on me."

Owl shrugged. "I only saw a man talking to another girl."

"He was all over her."

Owl shrugged again. "I don't understand the whole boyfriend/girlfriend/monogamy thing. Cheating, to me, is when you take advantage of a girl. Like getting a girl to blow you and not returning the favor. Now, that would be a dick move to get pissed about."

I looked at him like he was crazy. Because that statement, that definition, was crazy.

Owl looked over at me and grinned. "I get it. You're a mono girl. You believe in monogamy."

A crack of thunder sounded from outside the car. "You don't?"

"I don't think it's fiction. I've seen it work for some people, like my parents. I just have no interest in it personally. But you do, don't you Kira. I should probably tell you to stay away from me."

I had planned to stay away from him. People tell you who they are when you meet them. My problem was that I rarely listened.

"But I won't tell you that," Owl said. "I enjoyed fucking you tonight. I'd like to do it again."

My pussy throbbed at the prospect. "I just got out of a relationship. I'm not ready to play any more games."

"Did you hear a word I said? I don't want a relationship with you. I want to fuck you. And trust me, you'd like the games I'd play with you."

He stopped the car. I looked out the window. We'd arrived at my dorm. Owl hopped out of the car and came around to my door. He helped me out and handed me a card. "Watchers Auto and Body," the card read. At the top it had a tire with wings over the lettering.

"Give me a call if you want another ride, Kira. I'd be more than happy to come and get you."

"You're not gonna come up?"

"What for? It's late. I'm tired. I'm gonna head home and get some sleep. I hope you call, Kira." And with that, he took off into the night.

Up in the sky, the storm clouds were rolling away. They'd never even broken. I looked down at the card in my hand. I should leave it on the pavement. This guy wasn't boyfriend material. He didn't believe in monogamy. He'd said he liked fucking women and sharing them with his boys. This was definitely not the kind of relationship I needed in my life.

I stood outside for long moments twirling the card between my fingers. Finally, I turned towards my dorm. With each step I took my pussy throbbed at the absence of Owl buried deep inside of me. For the first time, it wasn't a painful ache. It was twinges of longing. I held the card in the palm of my hand and made my way inside.

When I got to my door, Sergio was there waiting.

"What are you doing here?" I said.

"I wanna talk," he said.

Even from far away, I spotted the pink lipstick on the collar of his shirt. I shook my head. "I don't want to talk to you."

"Did you fuck him? That chink?"

"You're a racist asshole. And your ignorant as

well because he's Japanese, not Chinese…I think. And yeah, I did fuck him. And it was a good fuck. A really good fuck."

Sergio's face went beet red. "Well, I fucked that blonde too."

"Good for you." I shrugged, turning the key into the lock of my door. I felt another twinge in my pussy at the sound, reminding me of Owl unlocking my orgasm.

"Wait, Kira. You don't want me to come in? You gonna send me out into the night? There's a storm coming."

"The storm already passed, Sergio." I went in and closed the door in his face.

I took out Owl's card. I programmed the number into my phone. But instead of hitting Save, I hit Talk.

The phone rang.

I panicked.

Before I could hang up, he answered. "Hello?"

I gulped. "Hey, Owl. I was just putting your number in my phone and hit Talk instead of Save and-"

"You in your room?"

"Y-Yes."

"Me, too."

"You got home fast."

He chuckled. "I drive a race car. You alone?"

"Yeah."

"Me, too. Take off your panties."

My hand shook as I held the phone to my cheek. It felt like I was about to cross some invisible line.

"Kira," there was steel in his soft, calm voice. "Take off your panties and go lay down on your bed."

My feet moved to the beat of my throbbing pussy. The bed creaked under my weight as I sat down.

"Good girl," he said. "Put your fingers in your mouth. Get them good and wet."

He waited while I did as he asked.

"Now, spread your thighs..."

Will Kira give Owl total control?
Of course she will!
But at what cost?
To find out, get the full story!

Read Cruise Control, Book 2 in the Watchers Crew series.

CRUISE CONTROL IS **the second book in the Watchers Crew series; a scorching hot, urban erotic romance series that explores themes of domination, menage, and open relationships.**

If you like your heroes alpha and multiple, then you'll love the men of the Watchers Crew.

Buy *Cruise Control* today and explore a world where there's always a happy ending, but it's shared.

ALSO BY INES JOHNSON

Lover of fairytales, folklore, and mythology, Ines Johnson spends her days reimagining the stories of old in a modern world. She writes books where damsels cause the distress, princesses wield swords, and moms save the world.

You can sign up for her mailing list and receive alerts and free reads at http://bit.ly/InesReaders.

The Watchers Crew

Test Drive

Cruise Control

Dangerous Curves Ahead

Slippery When Wet

Smart Baztard

a free story in the world of the Watchers Crew available exclusively to

Ines Johnson's Readers Group.

www.ingramcontent.com/pod-product-compliance
Lightning Source LLC
LaVergne TN
LVHW012035070526
838202LV00056B/5506